TSAR

of the

EMPTY

LANDS

Through worlds unnumbered though the God be known,
'Tis ours to trace Him only in our own.

~

Alexander Pope

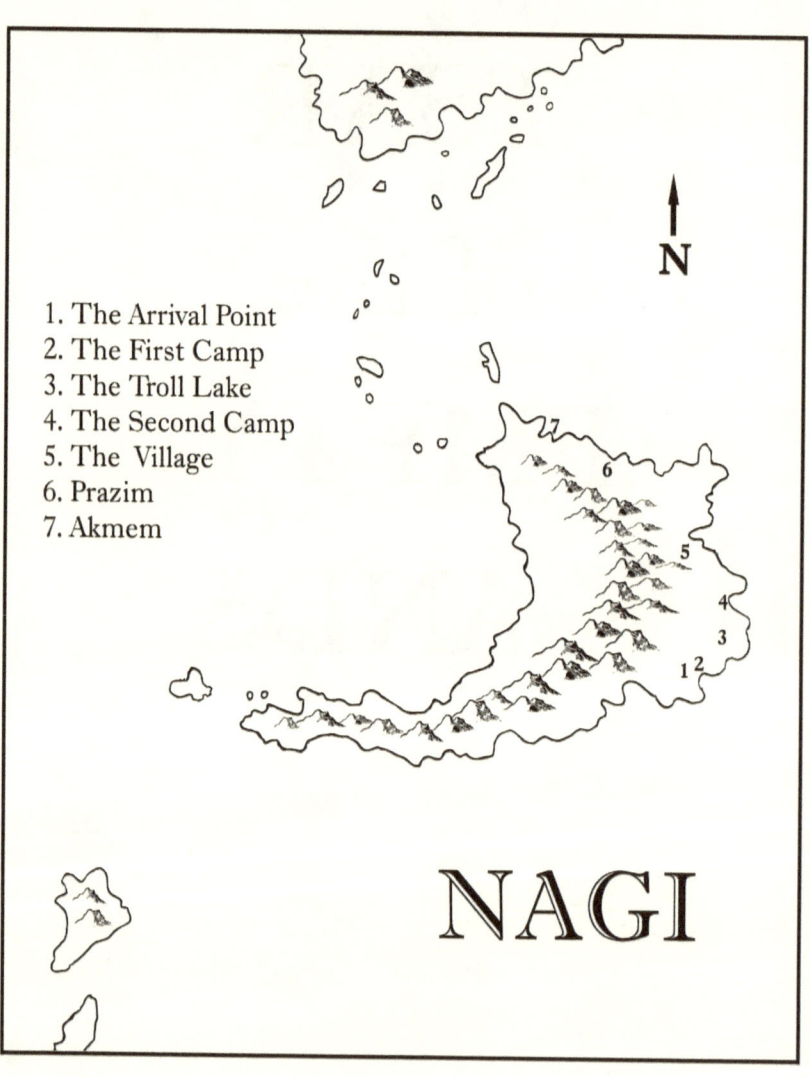

1. The Arrival Point
2. The First Camp
3. The Troll Lake
4. The Second Camp
5. The Village
6. Prazim
7. Akmem

NAGI

Tsar of the Empty Lands

Stephen Brooke

Arachis Press 2018

Tsar of the Empty Lands
©2018 Stephen Brooke

ISBN 978-1-937745-54-7

Arachis Press
4803 Peanut Road
Graceville, FL 32440
http://arachispress.com

Part I. Two Worlds

1. A Train to Siberia

Were I a better poet I might have been a prisoner rather than a guard. Too many had been sent to the labor camps, to the prisons, and too many had not returned. But I had no fame and drew no attention.

I knew not whether to feel cursed or blessed.

The lieutenant lit one his treasured cigarettes, breathed deeply of the smoke, and looked up and down the line of cars. "Over the mountains next," he said, before turning to me. "Any problems, Josef?"

"No, sir. Or the usual ones, I should say."

"Yes, the usual ones." The man sighed and pulled his greatcoat closer about him. The lieutenant was not a large man and it practically engulfed him. The train whistle sounded. "Off to Sverdlovsk," he said, and swung aboard.

And then on into Siberia. With autumn well advanced, it was not a good time to be journeying east. Maybe it was never a good time. Certainly not for the prisoners packed into these cars, men sentenced to the work camps. Yes, and women too. We didn't always have those on these trains.

Sossinsky disappeared into the troop car. I did not expect him to reappear, nor Starshina Rudakov. They would sit by the stove and leave the work to me. They might have a bottle, too.

Not that there was much work. There were three cars filled with prisoners, huddled against the cold and not inclined to give any trouble. Ahead of them, many boxcars, at least half of them empty. They would be filled somewhere across the Urals. That was according to government planners; everyone else knew better.

A guard was posted at each end of each car. The rest of our soldiers, only a handful for this duty, would be with the lieutenant and the starshina, keeping out of the weather. There was a man from the secret police, too. He spoke little but was in charge, none the less. It would be good if the police just took care of all these sorts of things themselves and left the army out of it.

If it weren't so cold, we might have posted men atop the cars too. I was not about to suggest it, even though I was the one to think of it. Best I check on the men. The prisoners too, not that I could do anything about them.

The man just inside the door came to something resembling attention. "Komandir," he said. I only nodded an acknowledgment. My rank is not so very high; in other countries I would be called 'Corporal.' Here, I am komandir of a squad, ten or a dozen men. That varied.

Last year, almost everyone was called a komandir. The lieutenant was komandir of a platoon. It was very confusing and we were all glad it was changed. I have heard no one had held the rank of lieutenant since the days of the tsars. I am not old enough to know for sure.

There was a faint light from a lamp at each entry. I picked my way through the throng of transportees. There were too many for the benches so some sat or lay in the aisle. No problems here. "Be careful, Grandfather," whispered the soldier at the other door, as I stepped out into the cold. "There is ice."

Grandfather. That is what the enlisted men call a soldier who has been in the army for a year and a half or so. My two years would be up soon. I considered staying in the army. Soon, I would be promoted to starshina if I remained. There is little doubt of that. I had been marked for advancement early; my officers recognized I was more able than the typical Red Army Man. Those were mostly peasants, or the sons of workmen. There is nothing wrong with that, I know. We are told so quite often and it would be unwise to say otherwise.

But my parents were intellectuals. When my enlistment was up, it was assumed I would enter the university, become a teacher somewhere, maybe. That held little interest. Neither did the army but it was at least a more secure life than most. As long as that German madman didn't start a war. I would be called back into service anyway, were that to happen.

Better to stay and have some rank. Ah, it was cold between the cars!

There was snow in the wind and the stars had hidden themselves. I stepped carefully across the gap and hurried through the door into the next coach.

There were women here. I didn't think I had seen any in the car I just left, but it was dark. What had they done to be sentenced? None of my business, none of my business. I shook my head and made my way down the aisle.

"Dobrov?" came a voice from the gloom. To my left — who would know me here?

"Erlich." Yes, Daniel Erlich. Hadn't he been off to the university? Leningrad, I was fairly sure. Not that I knew the man well; his family had been friends of my family and he two or three years older than I.

"I will not ask why you are here," I carefully told him, "but I am sorry to see you."

He spread his arms, indicating his fellow prisoners. "Be sorry to see any of them, Comrade," he said. It made me uncomfortable to be called comrade, but I could hardly tell him not to.

"We all have our crimes," he continued. His face was thin, his beard unkempt. He had always looked that way, hadn't he? It wasn't from being a prisoner. "Some are petty thieves, some are petty poets. Weren't you a poet, Josef? It is a dangerous occupation these days."

"Only if one is caught," I said, "as with any other crime."

Erlich cackled. "Oh, I remember what a cynic you are!"

Cynic? Maybe so. "I only know better than to seek trouble, Daniel. I must continue my rounds." I turned from him and proceeded down the aisle before he could say more. Daniel Erlich would not be my concern once he was delivered to the gulag. Chances are, we wouldn't even accompany these prisoners all the way. The lieutenant hadn't said anything about his orders nor their destination. Maybe he was as ignorant as I.

The third car was jammed even fuller than the others. "When will we eat?" someone called. It was an old man's voice but I was not sure an old man was behind it. Who could tell in the dark?

"Sverdlovsk," I answered. It could be true. I did not know. I did not bother to go to the far end, but only raised a hand in greeting to the man stationed there, my assistant komandir. There was no reason to thread my way through the bodies.

I should send relief for the men in a few hours, the other half of my squad. The lieutenant or the starshina would eventually think to change to the other squad. Perhaps not before Sverdlovsk. I was not sure how long that might take.

2. Climbing the Mountains

A very long way, I saw, when I studied the ragged map I carried. We had joined these prisoners at Sarapul and our last stop had been no more than halfway there. We would cross the Urals, not that they were so high here. That was probably why the railroad took this route. Beyond Sverdlovsk, I had no idea of our orders. This I have said before.

The cars stank. Urine, vomit, and other things I prefer not to name. Cold though it was, I was happier standing outside the door, on the open platform. No vestibule on these old cars. I could even piss out here, leaving a trail along the rails. But downwind! There was a storm coming, that was certain, and a powerful gale before it. Sometimes there was some snow mixed in it, sometimes it was wet. The train pushed on through it, ever climbing, but not so steeply yet.

We never crossed those mountains to Sverdlovsk. I felt the train slow, then grind to a halt. Men were ahead with lanterns, and I could see other tracks and switches. I jumped down, onto ground thinly covered with snow. Sossinsky and Rudakov were doing the same, and the police commissar came out to look down on the scene. It was dark but must be nearing dawn.

One of the engineers came back, along the line of cars. I could see curious eyes following him from the windows. "We are being rerouted southward, to Zlatoust," he informed the lieutenant. "I do not know why, only that it is ordered."

Lieutenant Sossinsky frowned and the starshina only shook his head. The commissar did not look any more pleased about it than the others. Maybe even less. "The storm, I would guess," was all he had to say, before popping back into the warmth of the car.

"This would be a good time for me to relieve my sentries, sir," said I. The lieutenant nodded absently and I went in to rouse the men. One short; I would have to tell my assistant to remain at his post. Dima would not complain. We both knew that extra duty came with any rise in rank.

So I of course would not be resting either. Should I say something of food for the transportees? There would be none around here; best wait until we reached some town. By then, they might be someone else's responsibility.

Our new route wound along the western side of the mountains. A small town appeared on our left, and a station, but we did not stop. Rudakov stepped out after a while, perhaps to check on me and my men, perhaps just to stretch his legs. "We will be passing through rougher land on this route," he said. "The mountains rise higher further south."

I think I knew that. "The wind does not seem so strong now."

"The mountains block it some, maybe," came the starshina's reply. "We will turn east and pass over them to Zlatoust. Maybe that way is better protected from the storm." He did not sound so hopeful, but Starshina Rudakov tended to be a sour sort anyway.

It was morning, according to my watch, but remained nearly as black as the night. Now the police commissar came out and joined us. He peered at the dark sky but said nothing. Not one for small talk was the commissar. "Any problems with the criminals?" he asked me after a while.

"None, sir," I replied. Maybe I should have addressed him as Comrade or even Comrade Commissar. I was never sure with his sort. "They haven't been fed in some time," I added. Why, I am not sure.

His face remained expressionless. "They'll get used to that."

"It is a hard life where they are bound," observed Rudakov.

"It is." The man pulled a cigarette from a dented brass case, held it a moment and then slipped it back. "Too windy," he said, and looked out at the dark hills for a moment. "Make sure you never have reason to be sent to the labor camps, Comrades. Soldiers do not do well there." There was the ghost of a smile, the first I had seen from this officer. "Nor do the police. It is the priests and other believers who survive best."

There was nothing to be gained in commenting on that. "The wind is getting worse," said Rudakov. No reason to comment on that either. The storm was going to hit us, despite our detour. My companions disappeared back into the troop car. I stood in the gale for only a few seconds before deciding to slip inside myself.

It was still hard to see much of the prisoners. They were undifferentiated shapes in the gloom, many with blankets pulled over their heads.

10

Were there enough blankets? I did not know where I would get more. We soldiers would not give up ours! "We are not going the same way now, are we?" asked someone. It was a woman's voice.

"A detour," I answered. "Bad weather further north."

"It looks bad here, too," came another voice.

A man's harsh laugh. "You are in a hurry?"

"A hurry to someplace with food!" spoke the woman. Where was she? Ah, over there. I could just make her out. Old enough to be my mother. Maybe she was somebody's mother.

All of these, mothers and fathers, daughters, sons. And now, nobody.

The car rocked with a sudden gust of wind. Gasps rose here and there but no outright cries of fright. Yet they were frightened; no doubt of it. I was frightened myself for a moment, but it passed. These men and women were already despairing, expecting only the worst.

"We should slow down," someone said.

"Go tell the engineers, why don't you?" rose a reply. Our police commissar would most certainly veto any such suggestion, be it from the military or the engineers. And even more certainly from the prisoners. I went on to the next car.

Almost, I didn't. The storm was raging now, the snow-filled wind nearly blinding me as I stepped cautiously from one platform to the next. The guard helped me through the door and shut it solidly behind us. I did not think I would leave this car for a while.

Hmm, Erlich was in this one. I did not want to talk with him. Not because I disliked him — I was fairly indifferent there — but because I wanted nothing to do with what placed the man here. The sentry and I both sat on the floor, our backs against the door. There was little else to do.

The train continued to shake and shudder. Could it be blown off the tracks? I did not think so but was not really sure. Other scenarios for disaster came into my mind. Snow-bound was the predominant one. Damage to the tracks, derailment was another. Collapsed bridges. Surely there were bridges on this route. But we traveled on, along the slopes of the Urals, the mountains sometimes rising steep beside us and the chasms just as steep below. I was thankful I could not really see those as we passed by.

3. Lost in the Storm

Yes, I dozed off. And, yes, I was on guard duty and could have been punished. It was most unlikely anyone would have come looking for me. I would have been awakened when the door was opened, too.

Something else awoke me. A rumble, a crash, a shaking. Was I in a bad dream, all those disasters I had imagined visiting me in my sleep? No, this was real. I tried to rise to my feet but the car was swaying too much. There were screams. A giant was pounding on the roof, huge fists delivering blow after blow.

"Avalanche!" someone cried. Then we were sliding sideways. And then not sideways, but forward, quickly, bumping and jumping down a slope. Then sideways again before we came to rest and slowly, almost casually, rolled over onto one side. The windows above me were already being covered with snow.

You are in charge, Josef! I told myself. "Anyone hurt badly?" I called out. I also listened for more falling rocks. None. Only falling snow, which was not much better.

Some was falling through broken windows. No one reported an injury so I turned to the soldier. He looked like a scared boy. I suppose he was a scared boy. Both of us were maybe. "Let's get this door open and see what has happened," I said. Oh, I'd better check my other sentry. "Andreyev, are you alright?"

"Yes, Komandir," came the answer from the far end of the car. "The door is broken here." That was the nose end when we slid down whatever slope we slid down. It should be mangled. I was glad the soldier wasn't, as well.

We peered out into the white landscape. The car lay at the bottom of a long and not particularly steep slope. A long dark scar in the snow showed its downward path. There was forest beyond us, tall conifers. Where was the rest of the train? I climbed atop the car and looked as far as I was able in all directions. Nothing to be seen.

Two cars had been behind us, one for soldiers, one for prisoners. Surely they had gone over the edge too. As for those ahead, who could say? Should I go search? There might be survivors who needed aid. With soldiers, prisoners, engineers, there had been around two hundred and fifty people on that train. But I had nearly sixty right here who were my immediate responsibility. I should focus on that.

So I told myself, though I was not sure. "We will freeze if we remain here," I said, and knew it was true. "We must move the prisoners." Three men with rifles. We could not really make these people do anything they didn't want. That they would want to remain here, I greatly doubted.

I went back in. "We can't remain here. I do not know what became of the rest of the train but we must seek shelter." I looked them over, those gray shapes standing silently — and sideways — in the wrecked car. "If you think you would do better to run off on your own, I shall not try to stop you. The rest, gather what you can and we shall go."

It was fortunate that all were able to go. There were bumps and cuts, but only one broken arm. "Stay close together," I warned. "You could become lost quickly in this snow."

"Hold onto someone," rose a voice. I recognized it as Erlich's.

"Yes, a good idea. Let's march."

Which way? I chose south, mostly because it was the direction the train had been headed. Any would have done, but my choice proved fortunate. This was rugged country, where the Urals widened, and I had no idea exactly where we were. Not in the highest mountains, that was for certain. Those would lie more east and south; we had been skirting along the side of them before crossing over. Here we were in something of a valley. Did anyone live in these lonely heights?

We had not trudged so far when we saw a shape ahead, one that did not fit the landscape. "It's one of the cars," breathed Andreyev. He looked up at cliffs. "It didn't fall as gently as we did."

No, it did not. It was all twisted metal, crushed by its fall. It was one of the prisoner cars, surely the one ahead of ours. There would be no survivors. Dima was in there, and another of my men, and seventy or eighty men and women headed to the prison camps. They all ended here.

But I had to check. How could I not? Some bodies had been thrown clear and lay stiff and grotesque, partly buried by the snow that still fell.

Yes, it still fell. I looked to the sky and saw a great darkness off to the north. The worst of the storm was not yet to us. A quick looking over of the wreckage. No one was likely to be alive in there and if someone clung to life, we would not be able to reach him. Leave it all to the snow. "Move on," I ordered. I must get these people to shelter before the worst came. None of us would live through that.

There was a rumbling. Another avalanche? No, thunder. Lightning played along the bottoms of the great dark clouds rushing our way. Winds howled about the slopes, among the dark fir trees. Then the storm was upon us.

The whole sky seemed to glow with lightning. Some could not keep their feet in the rushing gale, but others helped them up and we struggled on. Oddly, the snow seemed to have lessened, but it was still bitterly cold and these prisoners had little in the way of warm clothes.

Ahead — was something there? It seemed to be at one moment and then not. "A cave," one man cried out. Yes, a cave. I thought it was a cave. Large enough for all of us maybe. Shelter from this storm, at least, but the cold could still kill us. We made for it, stumbling through the deep oddly-lit snow.

I had brought them out of our disaster, all of them, and that was something. Let what was to come, come in its time.

4. The Cave

Was this actually a cave? It felt more like a tunnel, black, narrow, going deeper into the hillside. It did go into the hillside, didn't it? It almost looked like it stood aside from everything else but it was hard to see in the falling snow and that strange half-light of lightning.

A railroad tunnel maybe. No, there were no tracks, nor was there any sort of road. "Everyone in?" I called out. "Stay close together. We wouldn't want to get lost in here."

"Shouldn't it be darker?" asked Daniel Erlich. There did seem to be some dim source of illumination. I could not see where it came from. Everywhere, it seemed, but very weak.

"It is warmer in here," came a woman's voice. There were murmurs of agreement.

Maybe our bodies were just warming up an enclosed space, I told myself, but it didn't sound too convincing. And it was growing lighter and lighter.

All around us, the walls of this cave were fading, revealing a landscape drenched in sunlight. No one said anything.

Aside from the sun, it was not a particularly appealing land, rocky and sparsely vegetated. Scrubby shoulder-high trees grew here and there. There were, however, many flowers of yellow and of white, and some purple. There looked to be a large body of water in the distance.

A tall young man with a long beard broke the silence at last. "I thought heaven at first," he said, letting his dark, serious eyes sweep our surroundings. "But now, I think not."

"A priest," Daniel whispered to me. "Father Konstantin."

"Anywhere would be heaven compared to where we were," said an older woman. I think it was the one who had spoken before. She was short and full of body, though not particularly fat.

"Or where we were before that," laughed a young man, hardly more than a boy. "It beats being on the way to a work camp."

There were many mumbled assents to that. Then, one by one, these condemned men and women turned their eyes toward we three who had guarded them. I was glad we had not mistreated any!

But it was best I address them immediately. "I know not where we are," I began, "but wherever it is, I think we no longer have any authority over you." I smiled at the crowd. "We do, however, have the rifles."

I am thankful that Erlich laughed at that. It broke the tension. "We should try to figure out what has happened," he said. "It is rather obvious we are no longer in the Urals. Nor in winter."

That second observation hit harder than the first. A different place was odd enough but a different season?

"On the other side of the world maybe?" I suggested. "It would be summer in, um, New Zealand." I couldn't think of any other place. It was probably as good as any.

"So we took a tunnel through the Earth?" It was the older woman again. Not so old, still in her thirties, maybe.

I laughed. "Maybe so! It's as good a theory as any."

"But one I somehow doubt," said Daniel. I was seeing already who would be vying for leadership here. Wherever 'here' was.

"Let's see if there is any food in this place," I said. I tried to make it sound like a suggestion, not an order. I wasn't sure I even wanted to give orders. I wasn't sure I still had any obligation to these people, or to anyone else.

Was the lieutenant dead, and the starshina? Did it make any difference? I felt quite sure I was no longer in Russia, no longer any place where the Red Army would be a factor in my life. And I felt in my soul I would not be going back, even were it possible.

"Keep in sight of each other," I called out, as the group began to disperse. "Have either of you ever hunted?" I asked my two soldiers. Both shook their heads. "Just as well, maybe," I muttered, mostly to myself. "We should inventory. How much ammunition are you carrying?"

Aside from their full magazines, none. That was disappointing but not unexpected. No one would have thought it necessary. I carried an extra five rounds myself, along with the five in the rifle. That still wasn't very much. We all had bayonets, of course, somewhat usable as knives, though intended for thrusting rather than cutting. Orlov had a pocket knife. That might be more useful. "We won't use the rifles for hunting unless we absolutely have to," I told them. "Not until we figure out just where we are and what is going to happen." I looked from one young face to the other — faces only a year or two younger than mine. "Are you willing to follow my orders for a while longer? You don't need to anymore, if you don't want." Both Andreyev and Orlov nodded assent.

The hunt for food did not go well. In fact, no one found anything. "I saw rabbits," one man reported.

"Does anyone know how to set a snare?" I asked. I was surprised to see so many hands raised. Perhaps that sort of thing was what got some of them sent to a work camp. Among them was the woman who had spoken previously. "You, um, Madame," I said. "Do you think you could organize it?"

She nodded vigorously. "Call me Anna. Anna Levina." She motioned and a handful of men followed her.

"Men often follow her," Erlich informed me. "She ran a brothel."

"So she knows something of organization," I said. We could use that. "It's raining."

"And no shelter anywhere," he replied. "It's a barren place, isn't it?"

"But far better than what we left behind. Far better. That cave was the shelter we truly needed."

Daniel considered this. "Perhaps it is so, Dobrov. Or perhaps," he continued, smirking oh so slightly, "we may decide we would have done better to die in the snow."

I could only shrug. "One never knows, does one?"

5. The Stars

It rained a lot in that place, not heavily but varying between a mist and a drizzle. In the night, a short night, it cleared and the sky was filled with stars — strange stars, forming constellations I did not know.

"The stars look different in the southern hemisphere," Daniel pointed out. "I am more ready to believe now that we have been transported somehow to the other side of the equator. Perhaps New Zealand, as you suggested, or Patagonia. See the lights?" he asked, pointing toward the horizon.

"The northern lights," I said and then, with a laugh, changed that to, "or maybe the southern lights." I fumbled in the pouch on my belt and withdrew a compass. "Hmm, yes, it says that is the south." I was not sure how much I trusted it in this land. I was not convinced we were quite where Erlich now believed.

I counted our band the next morning. We came to sixty-one, all together. Although rabbits had been caught, and some partridges of a sort, it was not nearly enough to feed so many. We ate them raw, for there was no firewood. At least we all had a little to stave off starvation. Something must be done, some decision made. By someone. I considered leaving, setting off on my own, or maybe with Orlov and Andreyev. I used their family names because both were called Ivan.

As I mused on these things, I noted the entire group assembling around me. Would there be trouble? Anna Levina stepped forward, apparently chosen to speak for them. "Komandir," she said, "we need someone to be in charge. You seem best suited, despite being, um, one who would have delivered us to prison." There were murmurs of agreement and a few laughs. "It was you who led us to safety. We would all be dead now, I think, without you." Louder agreement to that.

And disagreement could be seen in a few faces. There were bound to be those who voted against me. I might have, myself.

But so things were and I should act. "The first thing we should do is move elsewhere," I announced, getting directly to business. "There is not enough food here. I say we go to the water." I pointed in that direction. "Do any object?"

I might be in charge, at least at that moment, but it was best to ask such things. None raised an objection. It probably seemed as good a move as any. "Prepare to march," I went on. "Gather what you have and need."

Little though it might be. These people were not equipped for any life other than that of the labor camp, having only the clothes they wore and some blankets, a few small personal items. The Ivans and I were not all that much better. Our uniforms — we had not yet been issued winter gear and wore only our cloth service caps. I would have given much for a fur cap yesterday but it was not needed here. Not yet. Each of us did have a heavy coat and good, high boots; these were not needed now either.

Shortly, we were on the way. Was that the sea or a lake ahead? The land through which we passed that day varied little from what we had first seen, though it gradually grew more rocky. More rabbits and partridges and other birds we saw, and little dark foxes that watched with curiosity, making no attempt to hide themselves.

We all hungered, I am sure, and none knew whether food might be ahead. My thought had been that where there was water there were fish. This might not be true were that a salt lake ahead of us but it seemed the best gamble.

By what felt like mid-afternoon — though my watch did not agree — we stood on a rocky shore, looking out over a rough gray sea. Fish there might be in those waters but I had no idea how we could catch them. That did not matter so much for the rocks were thick with the nests of seabirds. Eggs, nestlings, the grown birds themselves — all these we could eat. We would not starve quite yet.

And there, on the wave-swept beach, seals. A rookery? I had read of such things but never seen any seal except in a zoo. We might use one bullet and have enough meat for a feast. "Gather driftwood," I ordered. "We can at least have a fire tonight." There was much wood along the beach.

"Be careful of the seals," added a grave voice. It was Father Konstantin. "They can kill a man."

"Yes, stay away from any pups!" called out someone else.

20

I pulled out my monocular and scanned the seaside. "I see no young," I announced. "No small ones." Some looked half-grown.

"Then it may be the mating season," the priest said. "The bulls will be aggressive. I have seen them on the shores of the Sea of Okhotsk." I think there was something of a smile behind that beard when he added, "Yes, Komandir, I was an exile there. This was not my first time to be in trouble with the authorities."

"There seems to be no authority here but ourselves," I answered. But there must be men somewhere, no how matter how remote this place might be. I would be happy to hand myself over to whoever was in charge.

And claim asylum. I make no claim of having a great love for Mother Russia. Leave that to others. "Let's see if we can find some eggs," I said.

"And we should set more snares," called out Anna Levina. I nodded an agreement to that and left it to her.

"Let's go down and get a closer look at those seals," I said to Orlov. Andreyev I ordered to stay above and keep an eye out for any dangers.

"Yes, Komandir," he replied and even made a sketchy salute. Orlov and I worked our way down the shallow slopes toward the beach. I could see members of our party here and there, raiding the bird nests. What they might gather would help but was hardly a permanent solution to the problem of food. I wanted to look at the sea. Was it some southern reach of the Atlantic or Pacific?

There was nothing much to see. Little black and white birds waded along the edge, sometimes diving into water and swimming away. Some sort of puffin or penguin, I decided. Penguins if we were in the southern hemisphere. The seals mostly ignored us. The bulls were busy fighting each other when they were not busy mating.

Large seals they were, not the sleek little sea lions I had seen at the zoo, the sort that are trained to do tricks for man's amusement. One of these bulls might readily kill a man. All at once, they began to scatter, flopping toward the water at surprising speed. Even the largest bulls.

Something was loping down the beach toward us. Something danger-ous, I was certain! "Run," I cried out, though I doubted either of us could run quickly enough. I unslung my rifle, ready to give Orlov a chance for escape. But the boy had not run, and aimed his rifle beside me. A bear, that was what it was, and we were its target now, with the seals all fled before it.

I did not realize how large it was until it reared up. The beast stood easily four meters high. We both fired into its breast, and worked our bolts to bring another round into the chamber. This had become second nature to me by now, but Orlov had not been a soldier so long or perhaps he was simply slower by nature. He never got off a second shot. I moved to my right, fired again into the shaggy side of the bear as it turned and swung a huge clawed paw at the boy, fumbling with his rifle. Down went Orlov; a moment later, massive jaws were shaking his body.

Again, I shot. The barrel of my rifle was practically against the creature's side. It was definitely hurt this time. A fourth round into its chest as it turned toward me ended it. The huge red-brown body collapsed onto the sand.

Beneath those strange stars that night, piling rocks over him, we buried the first victim of this land. I feared he would not be the last.

6. Another World

"No bear like that roams the world," spoke Daniel Erlich.

"Not for many thousands of years." This came from Konstantin. Apparently, he was not one of those believers who rejected modern science.

This confirmed what I had suspected. "So we are in another world."

The priest nodded in agreement; Daniel seemed skeptical but offered us no alternative.

"Some of the uneducated have wild ideas about it," he said.

"Purgatory. The realm of the fairies. I have heard these," said Konstantin.

I smiled at these though I was not completely willing to discount them. "I've heard of no giant bears in either place. At least it provided food for us."

At the cost of five precious cartridges, a quarter of our total. We should make ourselves some other weapons. Spears, perhaps. I chewed on a piece of bear meat and thought on this. One of the men claimed to know something of hides and was going to cure the bear skin for us. That might be useful, in time. If this place were as close to the south pole as it seemed, it would become very cold. We needed to go elsewhere, find human habitations, if possible. I was not certain such existed here, now.

But this was not so bad a place to camp for a few days, to get our strength back, to prepare for what might come. Then, perhaps, follow the shoreline north. Here, the coast faced to the southeast.

No wood we found seemed suitable for weapons. This bear, though — his bones might prove useful. A femur could be sharpened into a small spear of sorts. The teeth, it seemed to me, should be useful for something but I could not think what.

We had sat without speaking for some time before Erlich said, "Do you suppose we could have found our way to a different time rather than a different world? What if we were now thousands of years in the past?"

"It might explain the bear," admitted Konstantin.

"Or thousands of years in the future. It is still a different world," I pointed out.

There was no answer to that. "Would you wish to carry the extra rifle, Father Konstantin?" I asked, after a while. He only shook his head.

"Me neither," volunteered Daniel. I might have asked him, eventually. Not before I had asked some others. "Maybe someone here has served in the army."

"I'll ask," promised the priest.

It was likely there were former soldiers among our group. Many serve for their two years when young. I would have liked the priest to take the rifle, though. He had some authority here, just as who he was. Best he be seen as working with me.

I might have even given him ammunition.

A little later, as it grew dark — that was late at this latitude and season — Levina came and sat beside me. "Now that we have full stomachs," she began, "men's minds may move on to other pleasures."

"Women. I have had that thought too." And had thought about some of the women. No need to mention that. "There are four men to each woman here."

"Some of those men are not so good. They truly deserved to go to the labor camps."

I was not sure anyone deserved it. I was not sure anyone deserved anything, for that matter. Punishment was a matter of expediency, mostly. "Criminals," I said, and no more.

Anna laughed. It was a curt laugh, like a bark. "I suppose I am a criminal. It was not the first time I was arrested for, ah, running a business. This time the judge decided I had not learned my lesson before." She shrugged and gave a crooked smile. "I think he was right."

I nodded. "I believe, Anna Levina, you may be the most useful person in this troop. Most useful to me. You know these people better than anyone." I would not allow Father Konstantin and Daniel Erlich to claim the roles of advisors, seconds in command. However much they might believe themselves deserving.

"I know some are political prisoners," she said, "like your two friends."

"Not my friends," I assured her.

"Hmm, no, I suppose they are not. But they have brains and are useful, eh?"

"Exactly. As you, Anna."

"Ho, then I am not your friend, either?" She smiled broadly as she said this.

I answered seriously. "I have not decided."

"That is wisdom, Komandir."

"Call me Josef. I think it is time I left my Red Army rank behind." I should tell the entire group this. Maybe in the morning.

"They will want some title to call you by," she said, jerking her head toward our band, most settled down to sleep. "You are our leader, like it or not."

"They can call me Tsar for all I care."

"Ah, then I must be a countess!" She rose and curtsied. "Your highness."

"And Konstantin shall be patriarch of our church," I said, falling in with the jest. "The Orthodox Church of the Empty Lands."

Anna sobered at those words and stared down at me. "Do you think this land is truly empty? Are we the only ones here?"

I spread my arms. "We can only go and look."

"I suppose so." The woman barely whispered this. "I'll go look for some sleep."

As should I. Yet I lay awake for some time, watching the lights play along the horizon. A few days of rest and then we would march north. Who could know what we would find?

I rolled over and left that question for later.

7. Steam

Before we left that place we killed one of the seals, a young bull. He had been hurt in the fighting and was not too difficult to slay with our primitive bone spears and clubs. I did not need to waste any ammunition, though I stood guard with my rifle as they slaughtered it. The meat we carried with us, and the hide. It was hard to cut up; our bayonets were quite inadequate to the job. They were all we had.

Some thought we should stay there as long as the seals did, and have a source of food. But that would do none of us good in the long term. We must learn where we were and prepare for a winter that would surely come in its time.

I let Anna pick a man for the extra rifle, an older fellow named Anton. By this time we were all calling one another by our given names — the families to which we had belonged were far behind us, most now realized. Wives would never be seen again, nor children. It was as if they did not exist.

And we did not exist either, back in the Soviet Republic. What had the authorities made of our empty car? What would they believe happened? Lost in the storm, perhaps they would say, and surely dead.

Anton had been a soldier. He had fought in the war against Poland. "We used these same rifles then," the man said, turning the Mosin Nagant over in his calloused hands. I allowed him the four cartridges that had remained in Orlov's magazine.

What Anton had done to be sentenced to the labor camps, I did not know. I would trust Anna in this.

We had seen no bears but more most certainly roamed this land. It would be difficult to defend this column of mostly unarmed humans if one chose to attack. Konstantin felt the one we had slain ruled over its own territory which was why no others had appeared. Now we were leaving that territory.

The priest knew much of natural history. He had studied it at some university or another before choosing the priesthood.

Many small, swift, cold streams were crossed as we marched northward, always in sight of the coast. Off to our left, to the west, the land rose higher, perhaps into mountains in the distance. It was hard to be sure of that. There were berry bushes along the way. I thought they were berries, but did not bother to ask Konstantin. They were still in blossom so it did not matter. Each night we set snares and caught a few rabbits. Sometimes the cunning little foxes found them first and we had only a part of a rabbit — and not the better part.

It was on the fourth day, as we made our camp, that I noted Daniel gazing toward the northwest. I could see nothing there to interest him, only the same low rocky hills, partially hidden by a fog. He laughed when I told him this.

"But what causes that fog, Josef?" he asked.

I could come up with a few explanations, which might or might not have been valid. I did know it had to have something to do with water. "We should investigate tomorrow," I said. It would be but a little out of our way.

By noon the next day we came upon a little lake nestled among the rocks and fed by a hot spring. "There is good shelter here," offered Anton, leaning on his rifle and looking the place over. "One could winter in such a spot."

"If there were enough food." To our group I called out, "We camp here. Bathe if you wish." I gestured toward the steaming water. It had not felt too hot to me.

Summer might be on these empty lands but it was not really warm. Nights were almost chilly. I would welcome a few minutes in that lake. First, I had to oversee the setting up of camp. A leader has duties. Others, without duties, were stripping and plunging into the pool. The stripping was to various degrees. It was not for me to attempt to impose modesty.

Father Konstantin did not appear eager to do so either. I wondered how many here might be believers, clinging to the old Christian faith, or some other faith, for that matter. Daniel was Jewish, of course, but his family believed only in Marxism. That hadn't done him much good.

I hadn't asked but it was surely his writing that got him in trouble. It was a lesson he didn't seem able to learn. His mouth might still be his undoing, even here. Others in our band? I had been afraid to ask, I admit. Anna knew as much of them as anyone. She and Konstantin. Some were criminals of one stripe or another. Some were political prisoners. Some has simply been victims, men and women who ran afoul of someone in authority or were swept up with acquaintances and friends who had come under suspicion. Not a bit of that mattered anymore, except for the few who had a record of violence. I trusted Anna to warn me of those.

I decided to reconnoiter and called Andreyev to me. Ivan I called him now, with Orlov gone, though there were at least three Ivans among the former prisoners. Up onto the rocks surrounding this hidden retreat we went and all the way around. I could see steam rising in another spot off to the west. There must be more hot springs. Perhaps it was an area of volcanism.

Looking down, I saw at least half my people splashing in the water. Yes, my people. I might as well call them that. This place was not big enough for such a group, certainly not for wintering over. Ten or even twenty might be comfortable here; not sixty. Maybe there were larger springs further along our way. We would move on tomorrow — or maybe the day after. I could use a day of rest.

What was that moving over there? I put a hand on Ivan's shoulder, pointed. "Men?" he whispered.

"I — think so," I replied. They were man-shaped, more or less. Surely not apes. They looked small but from this distance it was hard to be certain. Five — no six — of them were creeping down through the rocks above the lake.

One thing I could see for sure — they held spears in their hands.

8. A Tribe of Trolls

"Anton!" I yelled. When the man looked up I gestured toward our visitors. I wasn't positive he could see them from his vantage. "Stand ready!"

There was no need. The men, or whatever they were, immediately fled back up the rocky slope. Had they intended harm or were they merely curious? Maybe this hot spring was their home. Whatever the case might be, we would have to stand watch this night.

And we were not alone. Now we knew. "Primitives," I said to my 'council' that evening. The council consisted of anyone who wanted to sit and talk with me but almost always included Daniel and Konstantin and, usually, Anna. "Armed only with spears," I continued, "and they appeared to be naked."

"As were some of us," noted Daniel. "And I am fairly certain a few slipped away to engage in primitive practices."

"To be expected, I suppose," said the priest.

I could only nod agreement to that. "Maybe so, but a pregnancy would be unwelcome at this point."

Anna frowned at that thought. "One will come sooner or later. More than one, most likely."

"We had better be settled somewhere by then," I told them. "Peaceably, I hope, but with so many men and so few women it might not be."

"Maybe we shall have to practice polyandry," said Daniel. "Multiple husbands for each woman." He was probably jesting.

Konstantin, however, addressed the idea seriously. "The Lord would understand, I think," he said. "It would still be marriage."

"Or I could just organize all the women into a brothel and make you men pay to visit us," laughed Anna.

"And what would we use for money?" Daniel asked. He could be sensible.

"Oh, our Tsar Josef can make all the money he wants. He could declare this —" She picked up a pebble. "To be one ruble in his realm."

I had to smile at that. But, becoming serious, I said, "Our commodities here are food and hides. And our women themselves — they are more valuable than anything else."

"It is well you noticed that," said Anna.

I thought on these things some after they had left me. It seemed I did much of that these nights. We would have to find a place and would have to arrange our society in some way, make it workable. But I yet had hopes we would meet other men. Civilized men.

It was still dark when Ivan shook me awake. "Boris has disappeared," he whispered. I did not know which Boris he meant. I knew there was more than one in our troop. "He was on guard duty," the boy went on.

Maybe one of the women had distracted him. Maybe he had fallen asleep. We must find out. "Who among us knows anything of tracking?" I asked. I knew we had men who had experience of the forests. Poachers, if nothing else.

"Anton," came the immediate reply. "I'll wake him."

"Tell him to bring his rifle," I called after him. I prepared my own.

Leaving Ivan and his weapon to protect our group, Anton and I scouted the area where Boris should have been standing sentry. His post had been at the western end of our camp, near the lake. I could see nothing but after a time my companion pointed to the ground. "A scuffle here, I think. Yes, and something dragged that way." He pointed up the shore of the pool.

I could see this track, once he had brought it to my attention, and follow it. Soon, I could also see blood on that track. Neither of us commented on it. Past the lake and onto the rocky slopes beyond we followed. I was becoming uncomfortable with being so far from the camp, and in a place attackers could conceal themselves. Yesterday's visitors were very much on my mind.

Time to go back, I decided, but before I voiced it, we came upon Boris. It could only be Boris though he was not recognizable. The man had been crudely butchered; there was little left but offal and gnawed bones. Without speaking, Anton and I backed away and made haste to return to camp. Both of us, I am sure, looked back over our shoulders from time to time.

Cannibals. If they were human, that is. I was not certain of that. We roused the camp, saying only that there was danger and we must leave at once. There was grumbling, to be sure, and some were slow to act. But none questioned my command. It could only be hoped this band of criminals and complainers — most fitted one category or maybe both — would continue to obey orders, when it became essential.

The long half-light of the dawn was now illuminating the slopes. I could see more of those we had spied on the previous day. Where there had been half a dozen before, there now were a score and more. Again I scanned them with my monocular; I was closer this time and could get a better look. Men, perhaps, squat, incredibly ugly men with great noses like cucumbers and long shaggy hair and beards. Was that hair green or was it a trick of the light?

I pointed them out to Anton and Ivan. We might need to use our rifles. "Konstantin," I called out. "You take the lead. Get our people out this place." Others had spotted the approaching creatures now; those continued to slowly advance down the slopes. I hoped none would panic. Most had no weapons, no way to protect themselves.

"Get rocks into your hands if you have nothing else," I yelled, and then turned to see our foes at last charging. They had seen we were escaping. A few men with clubs or bone spears were standing with us. Our enemy was no better equipped, I could see, carrying clubs and spears as well. Small men — or something like men — they were, and their skins had a grayish look to them. Those skins were quite naked. The hair was green in places; I later decided it must have algae growing in it. But that was just a guess when I had time to think about it.

"Only I fire now," I warned my comrades, and took a bead on the leading man. The gun's report reverberated from the walls of the valley, possibly making the sound more frightening. Down went my target.

The others stopped at once, and jabbered at each other in a guttural monosyllabic language. Then a few started again to creep forward. "Do you have a good target, Anton?" I asked. He nodded and carefully sighted down his barrel. Another little man-creature fell; the rest lost their nerve and bolted back up the hillsides.

"I think they will not bother us," I said, "at least for a while. We need to get far away from this lake and from them, whatever they are."

"They are trolls, of course," stated Anton.

31

I shrugged. "Why not?"

9. Along the Coast

"I would guess that hot springs to be their home territory," I said. "Possibly where they winter."

Daniel spoke, his voice low. "More tribes may dwell at other springs." I remembered seeing the fogs that suggested there were other such places.

We had camped close to the sea. I think we all felt safer there than among the hills. "And maybe there are tribes of men somewhere. They may be no more friendly." There were nods of agreement all around. "If we had any doubts before," I went on, "I think we all must now agree we are no longer in the world of our birth."

"Then none of us will ever see the motherland again," came a voice from somewhere.

"I think not." This was fully sinking in among these people now, the people I led. *My* tribe.

"We must create more weapons." This came from Father Konstantin. "A man of God I might be but I see there will be a need to fight." Konstantin had been slightly peeved that he was leading our group away and did not have a chance to see the trolls clearly. They interested the naturalist in him. The rest of us would gladly have been further away from the creatures.

"We shall keep our eyes open for another good spot to settle for a few days," I announced. "Perhaps we can find another seal rookery or a place we can fish." No objections were voiced. Knowing they had lost their home, that they never might return to Russia — never mind how poorly it had treated them — was weighing on everyone. No, not everyone. Most.

Possibly I the least of all. Erlich had called me a cynic, but he was wrong. I simply never felt attached to anything. I did not care about these refugees I led, not really. It was a duty I had taken on, one of my own choosing. Without such a duty, why bother to go on?

And I would do it as well as I could. I set double sentries that night, though I doubted the trolls would follow us. Tomorrow we would move on, further up the coast. To where? Who could know?

One less we were the next day, without Boris, now not even sixty souls. Konstantin held a service for the man before we moved on. Some seemed to care about such things; all were politely quiet till he finished.

Anna slid up beside me as we marched more-or-less northward. "You should have taken charge of the remembrance," she told me, leaning in, almost whispering. "Don't let the priest usurp your position."

I did not think that likely and was about to say so. Then, a thought — it was not my position but hers she was concerned with. Anna wanted to be the one to whisper in my ear. Konstantin was a rival.

So, instead, I asked for advice, insight. She was glad to gossip; Anna had opinions on much of everything and everyone. Especially on those she saw as possibly being disloyal. Anna Levina had become my secret police.

Six days more we traveled, marching hard and long, before finding a likely spot. We stood at the south end of a wide shallow bay. There were beaches of dark gray sand and, yes, seals. Of humans, not a sign, nor of those that were near-human. I was to learn much later that another, even more hospitable bay had lain just a little south of where we arrived in this world, with humans living on its shores. But we had turned north and so it was.

"We'll camp here tonight," I announced, "and search out a better site tomorrow." The cliffs had appeared lower and the beaches wider a bit further along. But that was not so important; I wanted a defensible camp. We might stay for some time, getting ourselves ready to move along. We would, inevitably, move along.

There was a happier attitude in our camp, our community, that night. We found enough wood for fires. I decided there was no longer a reason to skimp on rations and so ordered. It was not quite a feast but better than we had eaten for a few days. I heard people sing and they were not all sad songs. Some were; we were Russian, after all.

People were becoming couples. That I could see and had expected. Anna and Anton were one of the couples; that, too, I had somewhat expected. I expected trouble eventually, as well.

There was so much we did not have here, some of them little things men and women become accustomed to. Scissors to cut our hair and beards, or blades to pare our nails. I, fortunately, carried Orlov's pocket knife, giving me access to the sharpest blade among us. Maybe the sharpest blade in this world. One knife only, but one knife could sharpen many spears. We would have to figure out these things.

Weapons, too. We had used seven cartridges, leaving only thirteen. The Mosin Nagant was a dependable weapon, rugged and accurate. But without ammunition, useless. I had already given our bayonets to other men to carry, so as many might be armed as possible. Attached to a good straight piece of wood, they would make spears. So far, I had seen no such wood in this empty land.

But the trolls had carried spears. Straight trees must grow somewhere. Somewhere in the higher lands, maybe, where I hesitated to lead us, at least for now. Better to keep tracking north along the coast.

We did so the next day and two more and found at last a good spot, a ravine that made a road to the beach. It also created a camp site with low cliffs on two sides which I felt a good thing. Not that I didn't think either trolls or men couldn't scale them readily enough.

The seals here were smaller ones, grayish and spotted. They seemed quite peaceful — the pandemonium of mating season must be past. I allowed only one to be killed. I think it was a half-grown calf, old enough to be on its own. Best maybe not to kill the seals that lived near our camp but go further along the beach. Snares were set for rabbits, as always.

We could fish here, I thought. The seals did! Someone would know something of it, of hooks and lines, or of nets. None of these we had. Maybe baskets. I heard of using baskets to catch fish. Somehow. There were plenty enough of the scrubby little willows growing in this place to attempt basket weaving. Those we used already to make our rabbit snares.

It was possible to survive. We could figure it out, share our knowledge. Share everything. Ha, we would have to be socialists whether we wished it or not.

Daniel Erlich would like that. He still believed in Marxism, despite all that had befallen him. But if he addressed me as 'Comrade' one more time I might just waste one of those precious bullets.

10. Visitors

We made tents of the seal skins. It continued to rain much in this land and shelter was welcome. I decreed that the women would have them first. Yes, decreed. There is no better word for it. It helped that everyone agreed with me.

We might need seal skin clothing soon. Summer was undoubtedly brief here. Though this was a good enough spot, I did not see us wintering over here. The seals and seabirds would be gone, and the fish and shellfish — we had found clams or mussels or something of that sort — would not be enough to sustain us. We barely fed ourselves now.

It might yet be necessary to go into the higher lands. There should be game there. Trolls ate something other than men who blundered into their territory. Another week maybe we should remain and then move on up the coast. I had scouted some ahead, no more than I could go and re-turn in one day, and found nothing of interest. Just the same barren country, the same empty lands.

I stood atop the cliff, gazing down at the beach, pretending to be ab-sorbed so none would bother me. Women, especially. More than one young woman had made advances. Some not so young, too. It would not be a good idea to involve myself, I was sure. Not even for a night. Maybe when — or if — we became settled somewhere. Then any one of them would do as well as another.

Gulls rode the breezes coming in from the sea. It looked almost calm today, and more green than gray. Far out, black forms, larger than the seals, broke the water and disappeared again. Whales maybe, though the shapes seemed not quite right. Whatever they were, we had watched them come and go since we arrived. None ever approached the beach.

A cry rang out from one of the sentries. This had not happened be-fore. What? Another bear? Trolls? I gathered up the rifle, always at hand, and ran toward his continued calls.

Two figures, silhouetted against the overcast sky, coming over one of the low hills. One stood much taller than the other but both were hu-man-shaped. "The one is a troll," whispered Ivan, who stood beside me with his rifle. Anton we had positioned further back, to protect our flanks if need arise.

I nodded. It was indeed. I raised my gun and pointed it toward the pair. "Come no closer!" I called out. The man raised both hands but his head was turned to his companion. He seemed to be telling him something. The troll backed up some distance.

I stepped forward but motioned Ivan to remain at his station. "Advance," I called. "Slowly."

A weathered man he was, with long curling reddish hair and beard, and clad only in a loincloth. A stout spear was in his hand, which he leaned on like a staff. He came within a few paces and spoke in a halting Russian. "You are come from the other world?" He looked over our camp with astonishment. "So many!"

"You came from Russia?" I asked and at once realized it was a stupid question. Of course he had. "Through the cave?"

He nodded. "I've never known so many to come through at once. Usually it is just one, as with me, or a couple." His blue eyes twinkled under shaggy eyebrows. "Was it a bad storm?

"A blizzard," I replied. "We would have died there had we not come here. However it was we did that."

"I am not the one to tell you," he said. "I am Leni." He looked a tad chagrined and laughed. "That is what they call me. They can't say Leonid." He gestured toward the troll, which was keeping its distance.

Unlike the ones we had encountered at the hot spring, this individual wore a loincloth similar to that of Leonid. "We had a bad experience with trolls we, um, met before."

The man smiled at that. "You recognized them for what they are, eh? There are some bad trolls further south, little better than animals."

So that was a good troll over there? I wasn't going to ask him to invite it closer. "I am Josef," I said. "Formerly a Komandir of the Red Army. Now the leader of these people."

He squinted a bit suspiciously at me. "So the Reds won, did they? I fled into the mountains to avoid being conscripted into one side or another, and ended up here."

So Leonid came through during the revolution, more than a decade and an half past. It was possible to survive in this place.

But how? "We have found little food in this land," I began. "Other than on the shore and we know that won't last."

"Had you gone south you would have found herds of muskoxen. Reindeer, too. Mug and I herd reindeer." He paused, looked rather thoughtful for a moment. "Someone, a man from the other world, told me once they aren't really reindeer. But they are close enough." He surveyed our group, as if trying to count them and then turned to call to his companion. The two carried on a loud conversation in an unknown language for a couple minutes, before the troll turned and disappeared over the hill.

When he was gone, I turned back to the man. "Mug you say his name is?"

"That's what I call him. His people have extremely long names only they use. Or can remember! I sent him to fetch you a couple deer for food."

"That is kind of you, Leonid. You own them?"

"They are the herds of my tribe. They took me in when I arrived here." He saw me look back toward where Mug had been. "Not Mug's tribe. Humans. We share with the trolls."

"Come on into the camp." There was no point in not inviting him. I turned to the crowd that had been watching. "This is our guest Leonid," I announced.

He followed me without hesitation. He did eye the three rifles; maybe Leonid had carried one himself when first he came here. Questions came flying from all sides. I held up a hand to quiet them. "Our visitor will tell us of this world in his own time," I said. "Do not pester him."

But one of the women had to ask, "Is it really another world? We're not —" She looked around a bit sheepishly. "In New Zealand?" So that guess of mine had not been forgotten.

"I do not know what land that is," he replied, "but it is not this land. You have come to a different world and that is all I know."

I suspected our guest was quite uneducated, a peasant, and moreover that the time he had spent here would have caused old knowledge to fade. He would have much knowledge of this world, however, knowledge we needed. "What sort of land is this then? Does the coast stretch on to the north?"

Leonid shook his head. "It is an island, I have been told. I've never gone all the way around myself. Many who come —" He thought about that and shook his head. "Many is the wrong word. Only a few ever find their way here from the other world. Always there is a great storm that opens the way. I wander off my path, do I not? Even fewer wish to remain. It is a harsh land and so they find their way to the mainland, to the north. I am told it has always been so. But I found a woman I cared for here and I was content to stay with her."

Daniel spoke. "We haven't enough women."

"So I see," said Leonid. "I am sorry for that. But," he continued, "you may not have mine."

I am not sure he understood the laughter.

11. By the Fire

There was no reason not to allow Mug into the camp. After all, he brought food, not two but three reindeer. Leonid was right; they did not look exactly like any reindeer I had ever seen. Larger, they were. Caribou, maybe, guessed Konstantin, or some relative extinct in our world.

Or perhaps that never existed in our world. There was no reason why it should, was there?

The priest could observe the troll all he wished now. Somehow, it didn't seem as repulsive as those we had encountered before. I am inclined to believe that was largely because it was friendly and not seeking to have us for dinner. The nose was huge and protruding, the skin the same grayish tone. But Mug's hair and beard were reasonably clean and had no green in them whatsoever. The body was barrel-like, the legs short but stout. He stood a little over a meter tall, about even with Leonid's waist. Higher on me.

The two jabbered in a language none of us knew. "I think I hear old Russian words," Daniel whispered to me. "And maybe Turkish." He sounded none too sure of that.

Both could have come through that cave or whatever it should be called. Had it been passing people to this world for centuries? Millennia? Forever?

And could more follow? What if someone figured it out and sent soldiers through, with modern weapons, with tanks? Maybe there would be some way of opening the door other than a storm. I did not like any of these thoughts.

It seemed I had decided this was my home, just as much as Leonid's. I felt free here as I had never felt free before. Ha, so I had gone ahead and loaded myself down with the responsibility of being a leader. That need not last much longer, perhaps.

The reindeer were tasty. Better than seal, better than bear. Maybe not better than rabbit; that might be debated.

Anna came and sat beside me, holding a rather large chunk of venison. "I wonder what the troll women are like," she murmured.

"If the men became desperate enough, they may try to find out. They might not care about their looks," I said. I had to chuckle at the thought.

"That is true. It is why I asked." We both stared into the fire for a while without speaking more.

"Whether human or troll women are ahead, we must make sure our men behave," I said at last.

"The women too. They will be curious." She regarded Mug, seated across the circle from us. "I wonder if that nose is the only part of his anatomy that grows so large."

"Konstantin thinks it helps the trolls breathe cold air," I replied.

"Bah, that priest thinks he knows everything. The church and the party are two of a kind. Trust neither, I have always said!"

I was not disinclined to agree. I was also unlikely to say so aloud. "I would keep away from any trolls of either gender till we get to know them better. And the humans here, as well."

Anna laughed. "Ah, Josef, those are the same everywhere. I would not be surprised if the trolls are too."

I laughed with her. "We need to learn their language, too, and soon," I said. "Hmm, it might be the language of only one small tribe and not do us much good if we move on."

"You see the worst outcome always! That is why you make a good leader." She sat back and gave me a most serious look. "Too many make decisions without seeing the consequences."

"I have guessed at things many times since we came here." Before, as well, it had to be admitted.

"Then you are lucky as well. And we are lucky to have you as our tsar!" She filled her wide mouth with another chunk of meat.

"Please, not tsar." I had heard others use it around the camp, jokingly. But whether meant as a jest or seriously, it seemed a bad idea. The man who wore such a title would be either too ambitious or a laughing stock.

"You said to no longer call you komandir," she reminded me, after chewing a while. "What then?"

"I do not know. Hetman?" That sounded unpretentious and maybe even a bit democratic. A hetman was elected by his tribe or band, was he not?

"Very well," she agreed. And then, slyly, "I shall suggest here and there you be acclaimed as such so it does not seem you chose the title."

I could only shrug. Let it be so, I thought. Over on the other side of the fire, Daniel and Konstantin were conversing with our guests. Or with Leonid who would then translate for his squat friend. Perhaps they were making a start on learning their language.

We should camp here a few more days and then move on. Move on and introduce ourselves to Leonid's tribe.

12. Making Ready

We had more visits over the next days, friends of Leonid both human and troll, curious about the newcomers. All were reindeer herders, apparently, out following their animals from pasture to pasture. Only a few could leave that task at any one time.

And apparently women did not herd reindeer, for we saw none. As for the trolls, I must admit I could not tell one from another.

Leonid promised he would lead us to his home when we were ready. The village lay near what was our intended track north anyway. We might have stumbled on it quite accidentally had he not found us. Or I should say Mug had made the discovery and led him to us.

Some made a start on learning the language. I was too busy. There were many things to make ready before we moved on, meat and hides to be cured, weapons to be made from whatever we could find. Our new friends — if they remained friends — had good enough weapons, spears with tips fashioned of bone and flint. These were a considerable step up from what the attacking trolls had carried, which were simply sharpened sticks.

But I would have been happy to equip my people with sharpened sticks were any available. It had to be sharpened seal bones instead, short jabbing spears and knives, shaped laboriously by rubbing on the rocks. We would not be defenseless.

They could be used for digging too. Things forever needed dug.

Daniel thought it quite amusing to address me as a Cossack chief. But he and everyone else did so in a surprisingly short time. "Hetman," they would say, "come look at this," or, "Hetman, what should we do about that?" I perhaps knew no better than they but I was willing to make the decisions.

Then came the sickness. It was not a terrible sickness, not life-threatening, but one by one we succumbed to it, a low fever, diarrhea. Yes, even I. What caused it none could say but we universally called it Troll Fever. It did come with our visitors, I suspect.

Perhaps we were fortunate nothing worse struck us. Or struck our new friends, for that matter. It would not do to spread disease to this land. "If individuals come through to this world often enough," said Konstantin, "they probably will maintain immunity here to the germs of ours."

"Leonid thinks fewer than ten have come since he did," added Daniel. "Not all survived very long."

Konstantin nodded. "A few are in the south. Others went off looking for a better place." The pair had spent the most time with the visitors, had learned the most of them and their language. It seemed the two had also become unlikely friends. At least they did not fight over women; Konstantin had sworn abstinence for the time being.

And Daniel found none to his liking. I knew there had been dalliances. He became bored with them quickly, or so he claimed.

Neither man had proven greatly helpful as a lieutenant. Yes, I sought their advice, for they had brains. As I sought Anna's. But to get things done I relied more on Ivan, on Anton, on other men and women who knew how to lead work. Several had been supervisors of some sort on farms or in factories. Perhaps such stuck out more and caught the notice of the police.

Or the jealousy of enemies. It mattered not at all now. I gave no titles, only asked individuals to direct some task or another. No one had formal power. Aside, of course, from me, and I might well lose that when we reached Leonid's village. They would already have a leader. And would I then remain here, herding reindeer? I could not help but doubt it.

What did they call their village? I wondered. What did they call themselves, or this island? So much to learn, but it could wait. We *had* learned — with a little help from our new friends — how to catch fish in the baskets we wove from the willows, as well as with line and lure. Many of those were now drying in sun and air, despite the fact that it still rained with great regularity, waves of drizzle passing over us almost every day. Was winter drier? We would find out, if we survived.

If we did not, it hardly mattered. The fish would help, as would the seal meat we were also preserving. We would not go to our hosts as beggars; we would have our own provisions, meager though they might be.

All was nearly ready, each problem that came had been solved in its turn. We could resume our journey, perhaps to a new home.

But there was the woman who dreamed. I must tell you of her.

13. A Shaman

Vasilina was her name. She was barely more than a girl, a poorly schooled country girl who had somehow caught the attention of the authorities. She would not speak of it. Some thought her mad.

Even before she began to have dreams they had thought so. More so, after. "She thinks she sees things," reported Anna. "Things that are far away, things that are to come." The woman sounded quite skeptical. None other gave the girl any credence either, but Konstantin worried that her statements would upset our people.

"Censorship, you want?" I asked him. I said no more but he surely realized I thought he was being a hypocrite. The priest considered my words and held his peace.

Not so Daniel. "It would be for the good of all if we asked her to be silent," he maintained. Daniel was rather obtuse for being so bright.

I myself considered Vasilina and her pronouncements harmless and gave her little more thought. I certainly did not believe she was any sort of prophetess or seer. Things changed when Leonid heard of her.

The man was not at all surprised, nor did he seem to have any doubts. "Ah, she is a shaman," he said. "The girl might never have known her gift in the other world, but here — here, people discover abilities."

It can be admitted we were amused by this. "Our shaman must teach her to use them when you reach the village," Leonid went on. "Those who do not learn to do so may be driven mad."

A shaman might not be a bad idea, I decided. He could straighten the young woman out and maybe teach her some practical arts. Shamans knew something of medicine, did they not? I should ask her to come see me, present the idea to her. When there was time, on the march. We were far too busy preparing at the moment.

The day before we were to depart Leonid and Mug returned. I could recognize Mug now, or thought I could. A third, older troll accompanied them, with a white beard that nearly trailed on the ground.

"This is Zup, a shaman of the troll folk," Leonid informed me. "He came to see your girl who dreams."

The troll jabbered in his own language to his companions. It sounded a bit like the troll tongue we had heard before but I sensed differences. "Zup does not speak my language and I only understand a little of his," Leonid said, when the shaman had finished. "Mug and I will try to help you understand each other."

Did I need this distraction at this time? Best not to offend these people if we going to be living with them. Or near them. "Very well, Leonid," I replied. "I'll see if the girl can come and talk."

"Call me Leni," he said. "It is how I am known in this land." I asked one of the men to go find this Vasilina, and turned back to our visitors. Zup gave another speech, which Mug and Leonid — Leni — discussed before the man gave me a translation.

"The shaman says he has sensed your woman. Her mind quests into other worlds."

I remained completely skeptical but was willing to play along. Vasilina came along in only a few minutes. Her first words, addressed to the troll, were, "I have been waiting for you."

This did not surprise Leni at all, nor the trolls when it was translated. Vasilina was a slight, plain little girl, her light brown hair falling limply around a pinched face. "You knew the troll was coming?" I asked.

"He — ah, how do I put it? He walked through my dreams last night. I could not understand him but I knew he wanted to see me."

I must not have looked like I believed it. That is because I did not believe it! A small crowd had gathered now, Daniel among them. His face mirrored my own.

The troll waved a broad, blunt hand toward the girl, beckoning her to him. She went without hesitation. Vasilina was either stupid or very brave I decided. Or maybe, indeed, mad. No words were exchanged. How could they be? But the troll nodded and spoke to Mug, who, in turn, gave his words to Leni.

"He is satisfied," was all the man said to us. That, and, "I shall return in the morning to guide you." The three turned and left the camp.

I regarded the girl for a few moments. I had noticed her before but not paid much attention. Green eyes stared back at me from either side of a prominent, turned up nose. Vasilina was both homely and attractive, in her way. "Stay and talk a while," I said. "It is time for the noon meal."

An uninvited Daniel joined us, but so did other men and women so I should not single him out for my complaints. But he did take a seat just on the other side of Vasilina. "I find this hard to believe," I told her after a while. I had to put some food in my stomach first, and wanted time to think. She looked like she needed to be better fed too. "But we have seen much that is strange already."

The girl nodded, somewhat tentatively. "Trolls," I continued. "Or just the fact that we are here at all. Who could explain that cave we came through?"

"It is a gate between worlds," she said, quite sure of herself now. "It takes power to open it for passage."

"You know this how?" asked Daniel.

She only shrugged. "I just do." She gazed into the distance. "I have seen other worlds too, and great —" She seemed unsure of the proper word. "Great sorcerers who dwell in them."

"It would be more useful to see our own future," he said. His scorn was barely concealed.

"I suppose," she murmured.

I wondered what Konstantin would think of us having a shaman to challenge his priestly authority. I rather liked the idea myself. "You must keep me informed of your dreams, my girl," I told her. That should nettle Daniel too, with all his scientific modernism. Some of it sounded as nonsensical as what this girl said.

Ah, for all I knew, Vasilina might not be speaking nonsense at all. Perhaps time would tell. For now, we had little enough time to prepare for tomorrow's march. Worry about all the rest later, Josef. Leave it for later.

14. Dreams

"My dreams were disturbing, Hetman."

For a moment I was irritated by the intrusion. But I had told her to report her visions, hadn't I? Vasilina had made her way up the line of march almost as soon as we had set forth. "Tell me of them."

Leni and I walked side by side, a little behind our vanguard. I had placed Anton up there with his rifle, and a few men with more primitive weapons.

"Trolls. I saw trolls attacking us on our journey." She let this all out in one breath.

I nodded gravely. "We are prepared for that." As prepared as we could be. "That could be no more that fears weighing on your mind, however. Nightmares."

I was a bit surprised that Leni agreed and even more when Vasilina said, "I know that. But you said to tell you." The tone was accusatory but with a hint of mischief to it. Then her voice went quite serious. "But I had another dream too."

"Two in one night?" I tried to make it sound like a jest but doubt I succeeded.

"I dreamed that a mighty man — a man like a shaman but more powerful — spoke to me. I could not understand the language."

"Another sorcerer?" asked Leni.

She nodded. "As good a name as any. I could see him clearly, a man with skin like aged ivory and a hawk-like nose. He looked young but felt very old." Vasilina fell into silence for a moment. "He did tell me his name. It was Hurasu."

"From one of those other worlds you mentioned?" If so, he was probably of no importance to us. Assuming he existed anywhere other than the girl's imagination.

Vasilina seemed uncertain but replied, "I think not. And I think he is coming to meet us."

Well, that would prove things one way or the other, would it not? It was to be hoped that this Hurasu was friendly. "I thank you, Vasilina," I said.

"Best you get back to your place in line. It is too vulnerable up here if, ah, trolls attack."

She laughed and fell back to walk near the middle of the group. "She likes you," observed Leni. "Maybe it is time to take a woman, Josef."

"Not yet," was all I was willing to say to that.

"Maybe so," came his amiable agreement. "I think maybe you like Vasilina too but there will be more women at the village." He chuckled. "Bigger and stronger!"

I think he was joking. One could not be sure with Leni. "If you have trouble with trolls," he said, changing the subject suddenly and without warning, "it would be soon. They are unlikely to roam much further north. Too many men up there."

Five days journey he had said. Maybe six. I assumed it was accurate — for him. It might take even longer to get my people there. This was my opportunity to work on learning his language as we walked. Others here had far outstripped me in that.

We would have cold camps. No firewood was at hand in the barren land we traversed, the same sort of land we had seen since arriving. We were no longer close by the sea so driftwood was out of the question. Almost all to be found for kilometers up and down the coast had been used up at our abandoned camp.

It could be seen from that camp that a prominent headland lay north of the bay. Beyond it? A rough and featureless shore, open to the sea, said our guide, sometimes cliffs falling straight to the water. Northwest it ran, to a deeper and more usable bay near his village. A harbor, it was, and men sailed some sort of boats from it.

I think the trolls, the wild trolls we had first encountered, thought us defenseless. We had no weapons to speak of — other than the rifles — at the time we had fled from them. Easy to ambush, perhaps, was their thought, and a good feast would follow. So they invited other tribes and followed our march. They picked off the first straggler before noon on the second day.

That was foolish, of course. They let us know they were there. Far more effective would have been to wait and attack at the end of the day or during the night, taking us by surprise. "Trolls are smart enough," observed Leni, "but they won't take orders. One got hungry and so it was."

Later attacks were repelled, now we were on our guard. We did not have to fire a shot. That sort of fortune would not last. Neither would our ammunition, but I hoped what we had would get us to safety. After that could be another day's worry.

Every person here carried some sort of weapon. It might be no more than a sharpened piece of bone but it was something. Anna had come up with the idea of sharpening the edges of the clam shells and most women had such an implement, small but razor-sharp, on their persons. Some men too. We had only used them for skinning animals or stripping willow wands so far.

"The land is rising, isn't it?" I asked Leni. I didn't want to be in hill country. I wanted open land where I could see who was coming.

"Some," he said. He turned, pointed to the west and then swept his arm north in an arc. "The great mountains lie closer to the sea here and our path crosses a spur. It is not so high, only hills. My village lies just a day or two beyond, sheltered from the frigid south winds, and we winter our herds on the far side." Seeing my look of concern, he said, "Fear not, these trolls will not go that far. They know better. If they attack it will be today or tonight."

"Where do your friendly trolls dwell?" I asked.

"In those same hills, in the many caves there." Leni seemed to take some satisfaction in that fact. Maybe he just had lots of troll friends. "That is good for it is they who guard the way."

The sun lay low in the sky. We were still in the summer though the solstice had come and gone sometime — it seemed we had arrived in these empty lands in the late spring. There would not be that much darkness to cover an attack. Some. I could spy, now and then, small bands of trolls furtively flanking our march. We would face more than the last time.

"Do they ever attack you herders?" I asked Leni.

"Yes, of course, but we do not go too near to their lairs. They are more likely to steal a deer from time to time." The tall man chuckled. "And from time to time we drive one or two their way just to keep them from bothering us."

51

"They *are* going to attack us," I stated.

"So it seems, Hetman," said Leni. "There are more than I can count out there. Trolls from many southern tribes."

"Just to try to make a meal of us?"

"Revenge too, for killing some of them and for trespassing at their sacred places." He laughed louder this time. "But mostly to eat you!"

"We need a defensible spot to camp," I told him. Soon.

"Ahead," Leni assured me. "I know the place."

I did not think that much of 'the place' when we reached it. There were too many rocks nearby, too many ways for an enemy to conceal himself. But the hill on which we would make camp was good enough, large and barren. "Half of you must be awake at all times," I ordered, calling out so all could hear me. "We will all try to catch a little sleep and leave again as soon as the light permits." Four or five hours only. If it was safer further north, as Leni claimed, we could sleep longer there.

I set Ivan and Anton to organize the guard, one to lead each shift. "Make sure everyone sleeps with his weapon at hand," I told them. "Sleepers in the middle of camp, watchers to the outside." There was nothing more to do.

None of us might get any sleep if an attack came. We might not even survive the darkness. Or some might and others wouldn't. How many would the trolls need to slay to satisfy both honor and hunger? I sat with the ring of guardians, rifle in hand, watching down the shallow slope. Dusk was bringing deep shadow to the low areas; I could sense the trolls were mustering there, preparing to charge. At least no rain fell at the moment to further limit our vision.

Were there more in the rocks, over there to our right? They could use their concealment to slip around us, surround our position. Even I knew that would be bad strategy. Better to come at us in one mass in hopes of overwhelming the defenders. But trolls might think differently. And then, a handful attacking from our rear after the main charge could cause chaos.

They did not wait long. Maybe impatience is as much a vice of trolls as it is of humans. I think some simply decided to attack and the others followed. Save for we three with the rifles — two at the moment for Ivan was stationed on the other side of the camp — there was no way to fight until the trolls were within arms' reach. I felt relief that none of the little creatures threw their spears but kept them in hand for jabbing at us.

I managed to loose two shots before, stabbing and slashing, the two groups came together. There was no order of battle. No, not on either side. Trolls pushed against humans, human bodies pushed back all along the line of battle. In the gloom, I could not see who might be prevailing. No one could see.

I clubbed at the attackers with my rifle. What else could I do? The best hope was that these trolls could not break through into the camp. We must hold them back.

And keep a line of defense at the rear, just in case, no matter how much we might wish to throw our full strength against them. If it came to the worst, those men in reserve might be able to retreat with what survivors there were. Was there movement in the rocks? More trolls as I had feared?

Yes, and now they charged forward — toward those who attacked us, crashing into their rear. Ah, there were men among them!

I heard Leni laughing by my side. "Yes, we used you as bait!"

Had I not been busy battling a burly little troll, I might have clubbed him right then.

15. Hills

To my amazement — to the amazement of all of us — we lost no one in the fight. I did wish our allies had shown themselves sooner, though, for many had wounds. "We had to make sure they were all engaged before showing ourselves," Leni explained. I still felt like clubbing him.

A few trolls lay slain. Most had run away without hesitation, making the victory largely a symbolic one. The trolls of the south had been taught a lesson; that was enough for Leni's people and their troll friends.

And we were safe. That was enough for us! But it would have been simpler had our new friends simply escorted us rather than play war games. Perhaps they grow bored in this land.

"These are not herders, are they?" I asked Leni once things had been sorted out. I noted that the trolls from our side were carrying away the bodies of the others. Were they cannibals too? I decided not to find out.

"No," he replied. "They came from the village and the hills to do battle. Now, we will all go home together!"

The trolls looked like trolls but the men were of a mixed sort. Some certainly looked Asian, but no more so than many a man one might meet in Russia. Others among them were quite dark. Had their ancestors come the way we did? If so, it must have been in a far past age.

Northward we marched, climbing into the hills by afternoon. I suppose they may be called hills but some grumbled that it was worse than crossing the Urals. And who knew whether a better fate waited on the other side of these heights?

One could see far but there was little to see. The barren empty land lay spread to the south. Not so barren and so empty as we had once thought, perhaps, if men herded their deer there and trolls lived in their caves. There were real trees around us now, conifers of some sort. "There is snow on these hills in the winter, isn't there?" I asked.

"There is," Leni said. "More than elsewhere for the slopes catch what blows up from the south. They will become nearly impassible through the winter."

"So you will drive your reindeer herds north before then." I looked up to see a large shape in the sky, dark against the high gray clouds. "A bird?" It looked like none I had ever seen.

My companion glanced up. "Dragon. It might be curious about us."

I had no ready answer to that.

We lodged that night in a large cave, humans and trolls alike. There was even wood for a welcome fire. Food however consisted of stringy dried meat and a sort of nut some of the men carried. Aside from being slightly astringent, the nuts were decidedly flavorless. "Acorns," I heard one of the women say. She was probably right. Acorns are a peasant food everywhere.

Leni leaned in while we ate to whisper, "Trolls will eat just about anything, including each other, but they're careful not to offend when we eat together. This is one of the caves we share along the route through the hills."

It was large enough a cavern they might be able to bring one of their herds into it too. But it would not do for living in, not in the winter. The opening to it was far too wide, too open to the elements. Too indefensible, too.

But I did not worry about that. Tomorrow we would cross over these hills and descend toward our new home. A temporary home, maybe, but more of a home than we had found so far in this land.

And my people might no longer be my people. They were subdued this evening, conversing quietly in the dark or already asleep. I checked our wounded; all seemed well enough. Some broken fingers. With close fighting that was probably to be expected. They had all been splinted. The worst anyone had endured was a spear through the side but it didn't seem to have hit anything vital. Others had taken thrusts in arms or legs.

I wondered how much damage we got in ourselves before the reinforcements came. Were any of those dead trolls ours? Not that it mattered, of course, but I liked to think we might have held our own.

No, it didn't matter at all. Trolls and men stood guard at the entrance, the remnants of the fire faintly illuminating them against the night outside. Briefly, I wondered how Vasilina fared, whether she dreamed. I could find out in the morning. I found an unoccupied space, wrapped myself in a seal skin, for it was chilly in those heights, and slept well and long.

Part 2. The Winds of Winter

16. The Village

There were larger trees on the other side of the hills, tall firs and what Konstantin felt must be ashes. I was disappointed that they dwindled as we descended. But no, our new land was not quite so barren as the one we had left. There were bogs here. Konstantin was most interested in those and yearned greatly to stop and examine one.

Sphagnum bogs, he called them. I know not one kind of bog from another. Larches grew around some. There were willows here, too, as across the hills, but more numerous, and what I thought might be birches. I didn't want to ask the priest.

But make no mistake, it was still an empty land, rolling and rocky, and covered mostly with sedge and heather. It was still a poor country to support human life. Could this village ahead take in another sixty mouths?

I asked Leni how many lived there. He could give me no number. "Very many," he said. It was Anna who explained it to me.

"He can not count beyond twenty or so. Between being raised a peasant and living in this land, he has never learned more." She smiled broadly. "But I would wager our Leni knows all his reindeer, even if he can't put a number to them."

Daniel concurred. "The people here may not think as we do. They will connect things differently. They may not think so much in terms of categories."

I had read something of this, some anthropological studies that focused on old, uneducated peasants. I had even seen something of it in fellow soldiers. "They see them more as stories," I said.

"That is poetic but probably the most accurate way to put it."

"It is safe to be poets again," I told him, and then could not resist adding, "as long as your verses do not mock the hetman."

Daniel laughed aloud. "You know me too well, Josef!"

Anna then surprised us by proclaiming, "I love the poems of Akhmato-va."

I am afraid Daniel sniffed. The grand lady of Russian poetry was not to his taste — nor revolutionary enough. But I was not surprised she spoke to Anna's soul.

I did learn, soon enough, that more than three hundred people inhab-ited the village through the winter. Fewer in the summer. There were also other, smaller, settlements not too far away. It did not look impres-sive when first we spied it, nestled in a valley where the hills faded into the windswept barrens.

Our trolls had left us, not continuing beyond the cave. Nearly three days more we traveled, as half a dozen men led the way down to their home, a collection of earthen houses, sunk partly into the ground, roofed over with soil and sod. There were more than I had expected, to be hon-est, but none very large. Burrows for hibernation, I could not help think-ing.

Leni's people surrounded us at once. Our arrival had to be a once in a lifetime event. More than a lifetime, maybe, if large groups never came through from one world to the other. I noted something about them at once.

"There is no cloth," I said. Everyone wore leather, some in loincloths, some in skirts, some in trousers. Long loose shirts were common.

"Nothing here to — ah, what is the word? Weave," Leni informed me. "I have not thought of weaving in many years."

"We will have to learn many things from your people," I replied. The sewing together of these clothes made of skin, for one. All the skills of surviving here. For those who chose to remain in this place. This land it-self might not support many additional human inhabitants.

"This is the center for all who herd the reindeer," Leni went on. "We will scatter through this land for the winter grazing, as we did to the south during summer."

"That is all your people do?"

"It is all I do, Friend. I would choose no other life. But some fish or hunt game or gather the fruit in season." His manner suggested good-natured tolerance but not, perhaps, understanding. "I am not one of those to venture onto the seas in search of seals or whales, nor haunt the high mountains, hunting wild sheep and elk. There are those among you who would, I think." He named no names but he was looking at me.

"Whatever provides enough food," I replied. That was what mattered. "We wish to do our share."

"What man wouldn't?" he asked. "Here are the elders now. Ah, and the shaman."

The shaman. He would want to see the girl. Vasilina. I had been too busy to speak to her or even to notice her. But first, these village elders. "Is there an overall leader?" I asked.

"A hetman like you?" Leni chuckled at the thought. "No, the elders meet in council to decide things. I could be one of them but would rather be with the herds."

I wondered what his wife thought of that. Ha, poor Leni would need to stay and serve as translator for at least a while. He would have to spend time with her instead of the reindeer.

Side by side, we stepped forward and greeted the elders.

17. Councils

There would need to be more houses. They all agreed on that. "They think not right away," Leni informed me. "Before winter, of course. More important to lay in more stores."

"Food," I said. "Clothing, too." My people were ill-equipped for a near-arctic winter.

"Well, of course," he replied, slightly perplexed. "The animals we kill for food will have skins." It seemed natural, I guess, to see all that as part of the same thing. A story, as I had put it, rather than food being something over here and clothing something over there.

And there would be dozens of other uses, for bones and sinew and things of which I knew I was ignorant. "We can camp outside for now, then?" It was even rainier than before but we had some tents of a sort. Leni gave my words to the council. I needed to learn the language soon. But I would not have Daniel or one of the others who had picked up some words here with me today. I wanted to speak directly with these elders, through Leni.

"There is probably room for all in the houses if each takes in a few," he reported. "That is your choice."

I only nodded. It might be wise to get the women indoors and away from the men. Give them time to sort themselves out here. "I'll have to see which of my men are suitable for what jobs," I stated. "I think some were herdsmen in Russia, but sheep, not reindeer."

"I drove sheep and cows a long time ago." Leni seemed to be lost in the memory of it for a moment. "There are none here but there are those further north who keep sheep. It is too mountainous for the deer there."

That was good to know. I wondered if those herders of sheep were friendly. "What about further south?" I asked. "Are there reindeer there too?"

"Wild, mostly. They keep no herds in the far south. The tribes there only fish and hunt." Too cold, too barren, I guessed. It was good we turned north, then, even if human settlements were closer the other way.

We sat before one of the earthen houses. A small peat fire smoldered in a ring. Eight men and women, elders but not particularly elderly. No, make that seven elders, and the shaman. He was indeed elderly, a wizened old man, and had not spoken through all of this. We ate grilled meat that was surely reindeer, and an acorn bread, and something akin to yogurt. Would it not be past the time the reindeer gave milk? I admittedly did not know. I would have to learn how they kept it stored. Buried in permafrost, maybe? Not this far north I would have thought but, again, I knew I was ignorant of such things — of many things.

"I am thankful that we are being greeted as friends rather than being turned away," I said. "We will work hard to repay you."

Leni started to translate and then halted. "There is no word that means repay in our language," he said. "I will just say that you will work as one of us."

Good enough. The elders murmured some sort of pleasantries in return, which Leni did not bother to turn into Russian. At last, when all had said what was to said, the shaman spoke. Only two words. "He asks where the girl is."

The old fellow was dressed as I would imagine an American Indian, in leather leggings and shirt. A conical cap covered a head I assumed to be bald, and a sparse white beard hugged his jawline. I could not say what race his features and color suggested; maybe all of them at once.

"Shall I call her?" I asked. A few words exchanged.

"No, Josef, he would like to go to her. We are finished here otherwise."

Very well. I rose and bowed slightly — little more than a respectful nod, it was — to the council of elders. "Come, then." The old shaman followed the two of us, not speaking.

But he seemed excited. Indeed, he could hardly contain himself. "Ati feared he would never have an apprentice to train," whispered Leni. "Those with talent are very rare and much knowledge would have been lost." He looked back at the old man. "He was much disappointed that none of his children nor grandchildren had the gift."

"It is inherited, then? Normally?" Not that I yet believed in this 'gift.'

"So I have heard." That was probably the extent of our friend's knowledge on the subject.

My people were sitting much where I had left them, for the most part. That would not do. We were no longer to be a tribe apart from our hosts. Before seeking out Vasilina, I addressed them. "I am no longer your hetman," I announced. "This will be our village and it has its own elders. Learn the language. Learn how to live here." No more than this did I say.

There would be more to say later; better to give them some time to think and talk first. I spied the girl and motioned her to us. "Vasilina, this is the shaman of these people, Ati." Leni made what was probably a similar introduction to the old man.

"Vasaleni?" he repeated, squinting at the girl.

"Tell him to call me, mmm, Vasa," she said. "Can he do that?"

He could. "Vasa." Ati nodded approval of the name, of the girl, of whatever. Then he gave a rather long-winded speech neither I nor Vasilina could follow. She had a little more of the language here than I, but not much.

"He feels the gift in you, he says," reported Leni. "You should come and live with him and he will teach you." He grinned at us. "The shaman's house is very big; he and his wife have many children and grandchildren dwelling there."

"One way to learn the language," I said. "If you wish, Vasilina."

"Why not? I'll get my things." Meager though they were — the girl gathered them together and followed the old man away.

"You must wish to get to your wife," I said to Leni. "Is she about somewhere?"

He laughed heartily. "You have met her, Josef. She is one of the elders."

I had to chuckle at that myself. "Ah, you have done well here then, Leni."

"This I know, my friend. Far better than ever I would have in the land of my birth." He sounded like a man very sure of himself. "Far better."

18. Lessons

"He is not a priest," she told me. "More like a doctor." Vasilina giggled. I think it was the first time I had heard her do that. "He's been taking me out and showing me where to pick herbs and telling me what their names are. Probably what they're good for, too, but I don't understand enough yet."

None of us did, but we were learning. It was a simple language. No, that is not surprising. I think it was a sort of pidgin, forged of the many tongues that had came through the gate, and those are always simple. It is when languages mature and when their speakers are cut off from others that they grow complex. Language had always interested me; maybe, had I remained in Russia and left the army, I would have studied philology. Or anthropology, maybe.

Now I was studying both, in the field if you will. "Priests are a separate vocation here," I said. "Leni's wife is priestess to this village."

"The woman I saw wearing antlers?" she asked. They were for some ceremony no one explained to us.

I nodded. "I can not figure out what god or gods she serves, however." The woman's name was Olga. Some Russian names had survived here. There was even another Russian in the village, an old man who passed between worlds decades before Leni. He could not remember any of the language he once had spoken.

"I think Ati is skeptical of religion." Vasilina's voice took on some of the dreaminess it held when first I spoke to her. "He sees things beyond this world."

That I found amusing. Perhaps I should not have. "So shamans are the scientists of this world?"

"Maybe so. He will teach me to see, also, and how to speak to other shamans from afar."

I was the one skeptical of this but I said nothing of it. Instead, I asked, "You are comfortable with remaining in his house?"

"Oh, yes, Josef. Already one of his grandsons has asked me to marry him!" She giggled for a second time. Vasilina could giggle all day and it would be alright with me.

Ah, would it? I wondered later. Better to not allow myself such day-dreaming, such sentiment. Vasilina would do well to marry a grandson of Ati, have a place among these people. I did not see myself remaining. I was no Leni, to be content following the herds.

But for now, I had an obligation to my people, to get them settled in this land. I had taken it on, would see it through — through the winter to come, at least. I was still seen as a leader by both our refugees and the villagers. Indeed, the elders apologized that I was too young to join their council. I suggested Anna instead; she now sat with them.

I did not know whether they regretted that. But Anna was good with words and had picked up the language more quickly than most. She was able to be a liaison between me and the council. That meant Leni could escape back to his reindeer.

"Yuzi," Anna informed me, "we think some of the men might be better settled elsewhere before winter." She called me Yuzi, now, as did the villagers. It was the best they could do with my name. Vasilina was Vasa, too, and others of us had altered names. Anna, of course, was perfectly well pronounced by everyone and already in the correct feminine form.

"I know there are other villages," I replied. "Or camps, maybe? We should know more of them." I should go see them was what I meant, instead of sitting around here.

"Anton thinks he would like to join those who hunt in the mountains." She was not ready to rename Anton yet, nor was there a consensus on what to call him in the village. "It would probably be a good thing." The woman did not sound too sure of it.

"I think he should not take the rifle," I mused, "not that it really matters much." We had all expended cartridges in the battle with the trolls. All together, only seven remained.

"He will be among those who go into the hills tomorrow to cut wood. Much wood is needed."

"Both for fires and tools." I knew this. "Perhaps I should go too." I could see the mountains rising to the west were topped with snow, even in midsummer. Surely there would be much more soon, and even more in the south where we had first arrived. Now was the time to go to them.

"You are needed more here, Yuzi," she told me. "Do not try to escape your real work."

"Digging holes for more houses?" We both laughed at that. It seemed to be my main job lately. Slow work it was, working the earth loose with an antler, scooping it up into a basket and piling it elsewhere. Some of the wood they intended to cut would go into roofing over those houses.

"Keeping our people in line," Anna said. "Everyone recognizes that you are the one who can tell them what to do."

"If they remain here they will have to listen to the elders. I may not stay."

"If you go, some will follow you. You know this, do you not?"

I did, though I had not thought much on it. "And not just our people," she went on. "There are young men and women here who yearn to find new lands. That, it seems, has always been so."

I had heard this too. "This place can support only a small population. Our arrival strains that." I shook my head. "Nothing can be done about any of it until spring."

"You are right, my tsar of the empty lands. But, ah, I fear the winter!"

19. The Bay

I did go away the next day, but not to the mountains. It was Konstantin who informed me of a different destination, coming to me in the shifting lights of dawn. "We go to the sea. There is a village there."

A place where some of the extra men might be settled was my immediate thought. My next thought was that I was probably right. "How many?"

"As many men as want to go," he replied.

"Let them get a look at it," said the villager at his side, a man dark and broad-shouldered. "Maybe some will want to stay."

"This is Mazi," said the priest. "He is a hunter of whales."

Mazi did not seem to like this description. "I am a man of the sea," he stated. "Sometimes there are whales."

"And seals and fish?" I asked, smiling.

A guffaw from the man. "Sometimes! The seals will be out at sea more now but we may take some."

It felt good to know I had learned enough of the language to make jests. More than a score of men — and men only, though I learned this was not always so — intended to journey to the water. Daniel had chosen to join the group. I think he did not know what to do with himself, having no particular aptitude for any sort of work.

Though there were plenty enough ways to make myself useful in the village, I felt I should see something of the land here. "I will go with you," I decided. I am certain everyone had already assumed this.

"Then let us be on our way," said Mazi, "and get there before dark. Are these all, Konosi?"

"So it seems," replied Konstanin. We set out across the rolling hills. The berries I had noted before were ripening now. I would not mind being among those who gathered them. As long as I was not competing with bears for the fruit.

I turned my attention from them and to the priest. "Konosi?" I asked.

"So I am named now. It seems a good name." He smiled faintly, perhaps a tad ruefully. "They were naming me Kanidi, which also seemed good enough until I learned it was their word for a louse."

"A nit, actually," broke in Daniel.

"Konosi is better. It means one who sees or watches or something of that sort."

"I can hear Indo-European roots in both those names," I observed.

Daniel felt that shouldn't be surprising. So did I. "Who knows what peoples have passed through from our world?" I asked. "There could have been Scythians millennia ago."

"Perhaps even Neanderthals if one went back far enough," he said.

I had wondered if our trolls could be related to Neanderthals. There was a certain similarity in build and I remembered they had prominent noses. Not so huge as those of the trolls, nor were they so short, but a species can change over time.

We marched on, frequently swatting at the swarms of mosquitoes. Those had been a feature of this empty land from the start, though never quite so numerous! Being next to the sea might have helped in that before. "Be grateful you are not with the reindeer herds," Mazi told us. "They attract even more mosquitoes. Biting flies too." I pitied Leni in his loincloth.

There were signs of volcanism along our route, hot springs and geysers leaving multicolored mineral deposits on the rocks. Nothing like the lake of the trolls, however. That would be quite welcome in winter. I wondered if it would be possible to drive them off — but no, conquest and war were never good ideas. Trolls had a right to their home. Even trolls that would have eaten us.

Then, too, it would perhaps send the wrong message to the friendly trolls.

With Anton readying himself to journey into the hills, I carried my rifle with four rounds, entrusting the other three to Ivan. Only in the greatest of emergencies should he use them, I impressed on the boy. I would take the same care myself.

Was it foolish to do so? There would come the day our ammunition would be gone. That was inevitable. Then we would need to defend ourselves as did our adopted tribe, with spear and ax and knife. Daniel had half-seriously made remarks about reloading the spent cartridge casings ourselves, but I knew the impossibility of it. This land and these people were not ready for such things.

We saw no other humans — nor trolls — on our march, nor any large animals. Only the usual rabbits and foxes, the several varieties of birds. That included larger birds, flying overhead, larger than I had spied before. I felt they might be seabirds, albatross or skua or something of that sort. Perhaps even osprey.

Konstantin might know but I had not enough interest to ask. I could smell the sea by early afternoon, for the breeze had shifted to the east. It might be that I belonged by the water, in the village we traveled toward, or some other. I felt an affinity for the sea, one I had not known before coming to these empty lands.

So I was to choose the empty water instead? Maybe, if only so I might cross it to some other land. When it was time.

There was still light when the bay lay before us. It was narrower, deeper, than those we had seen before — a true harbor. "From here north the coast is more broken with many long narrow bays, closed in by high cliffs," Mazi told us, sweeping an arm northward. Fjords, I thought. These people would have a specific name for them and I would learn it eventually.

The cliffs here were not so high and the way down to the sea was easy. No seals on the beaches could I see. What I did see, pulled up onto the sand above the line of the high tide, were boats, the first we had encountered in this land. They were of hide, stretched over a frame of wood and bone, and the largest looked as though it might accommodate six or eight men.

"I have seen such craft before," spoke Konstantin. Or Konosi — I might as well just call him that.

"On the Sea of Okhotsk, undoubtedly," came Daniel's dry comment.

They appeared quite flimsy to me. I was not sure I would be willing to go far from shore in one. What if there were a tear in the skins? And the water here was cold, bitterly cold.

I was having second thoughts about living at this village by the sea! The village itself was identical in construction to that we had left, the same earthen houses. They were not on the beach but set on and into the slopes above. Those who had come with us, most but not all from our own group of refugees, were looking the place over too, and some were having their own second thoughts, I am sure.

"Tomorrow we put you to work," announced Mazi. "We build more houses."

I had to laugh. "I just left such work."

"Then is not one place as good as another to do it?" he asked. "But now, we eat. There is enough driftwood for a fire?" This was directed at one of the local inhabitants. Both men and women had come out to get a look at us. The men looked less pleased than the already-outnumbered women. Some gave us quite unpleasant glares.

"Also," Mazi continued, "we maybe teach you to fish."

Someone said, "We fish for the deep bottom dwellers, far out from shore."

Our guide nodded. "Yes, it is still the season for that. We would not take newcomers out right away. Do not fear, though," said Mazi, turning back to our group. "We shall learn if some of you are men of the sea."

It would be good if some proved to be and found a place here. Right now, we were men of nowhere.

20. Itzo

Some of these people would remain through the winter. Some would return to our village or maybe some other. There was little travel between them in the dark cold months but some did make the journey. Those who remained — or only visited — needed houses. We all worked at those the next day.

Our excavations would be lined with stones. These were not essential but did help support the roof and served to extend the walls above the ground level. Suitable lengths of wood and closely-plaited willow branches, like a great basket, made a ceiling, the whole thing to be covered with soil built up around and sod on top. There were other roofs that needed rebuilt around this village by a bay, too.

We were well fed. There was much fish, some of it being dried for winter stores, but plenty fresh as well. I do not know fish. They might have been some sort of cod. Or they might not. I was told they were bottom-dwellers, caught on long lines, well out from shore. Though I was still leery of those boats, I thought I should go out and see it done.

There were one or two other fish mixed with these, usually, and sometimes a shark. "We catch many little fish at other times of the year," I was told. "Not so much this late in summer."

"Eels, too, in their season," said another. "And the seabirds when they return."

"And seals."

To this, Mazi added, "And the great whales. We shall have a hunt soon."

Now going after whales in those boats seemed even greater folly than fishing from them. I did that, a few days after we arrived; being recognized as a leader, I received the first invitation to accompany the fishermen. And, being a leader, I was magnanimous and insisted that the others go before me. Also, I wanted to see if any of them would drown.

The skin boats — I was in one that held a crew of three — went almost beyond sight of land. These people were not skilled enough sailors to chance more than that. They knew their limits and that is a good thing. We dangled long lines of some plaited material into the green-gray depths. I think it consisted of both animal gut and plant fiber, braided together for strength and pliability. The hooks were shaped and sharpened shell, baited with whatever scraps were convenient.

What did I know of fishing? As a boy, I had read Kipling's tale of boats on the North Atlantic and that was the limit of my knowledge. Yes, I can read English and speak it some. Or I could once. I was already losing it, surely, and would continue to in this land.

None the less, I caught nearly as many fish as my companions, once I learned to interpret the twitches of my line. I would pull hard, set the hook — or not — and then haul the heavy-bodied fish up, hand over hand. The next day it was back to house building and the other chores necessary to that place. I did not so much mind it there. I also knew I would not stay.

Near two weeks had we remained when Mazi at last announced his hunt. "We seek the whale," he told us, "but will take seal if we find them instead." All the boats were to go out, together. Our leader chose but a half-dozen from our group and I was one. Would that I had been more inept!

Should I take the Mosin Nagant with me? It seemed unlikely a rifle would be needed, nor should I take a chance of losing it. I left it ashore in the care of Daniel. Not Konosi — he was one of those chosen to hunt the whale. By hunt, I mean he and I got to wield paddles, I in Mazi's boat. Mazi and a few others carried long heavy spears. It would not be wrong to call them harpoons, maybe, except there was no line attached. These had heads of some sort of carved ivory fitted with a sharp flint tip. Those tips could be replaced readily. The weapon was launched with a thrower, made of antler.

Our boats did not go far out into the sea; instead we followed the coastline southward, on the lookout for any sea creatures we might take. A whale — or two — could go far in feeding these people through the winter. There would be more hunts until the winds of winter made them too hazardous.

"Seals," called out someone in a neighboring boat, pointing. Mazi shook his head. Too far off and swimming swiftly toward deeper water.

"If we see some on the beaches we might go after them," he said. I got the feeling he would rather find a whale. We found something else.

I thought it a whale at first. A dark hump — was it one of the creatures I had spied from the cliffs at our camp? "Itzo," spoke Mazi. "The shadow of the deep places." He showed no desire to pursue it.

"So far south?" wondered a man in the boat next to ours.

"They do not like the cold," said one of my fellow paddlers.

"And you know this how?" laughed the other before turning his eyes back to that distant dark shape. "Let us hope he does not wish to come and get warm with us!" Despite the jest, there was no laughter in his voice now.

"Silence!" order Mazi. He stood erect in the bow, watching the itzo, shifting the grip on his spear. It still looked like a whale to me — until its long toothy jaw rose from the waves. A crocodile? I knew not what else it resembled. "It spies us." Mazi spoke calmly, quietly. In all the other boats, men were readying their spears.

The creature dove, disappeared. Was it coming below us, preparing to attack? I did not get a good idea of its size but the itzo was not small! "There!" came a cry. The great sea-creature broke the water not too far from us, apparently having come in for a closer look. Maybe to decide if we were good to eat.

Not a crocodile. Even I, who had never seen one except in books, could tell that. The body was vaguely whale-like but there was a neck, short yet flexible. I did know whales have no such necks. A massive head with cruel jaws rested on that neck. The itzo's large round eyes glittered at us. It slipped beneath the surface again.

It must have made up its mind. "They eat whales and seals," the paddler next to me whispered. "But I have heard tales of them following boats and taking the men, one by one." I noted my companions making sure their own spears were ready at hand. At that moment I wished my rifle were not ashore.

The itzo shot straight up from the water beneath one of the boats, perhaps in hopes of knocking its crew into the water. I was surprised to see they all held on, but the hull was torn. They would soon be in the water anyway. "In on it!" shouted someone. It might have been Mazi but I would not guarantee it. As the beast resurfaced and rolled to see if its attack had been successful, half a dozen spears flew toward it. The itzo thrashed a moment and dove again.

The men in the sinking boat were rescued during the respite, clambering into other craft. "I see no blood," muttered Mazi, scanning the surface. He prepared another spear. Had the itzo fled, dove back into the depths to again be a shadow?

"There!" came from more than one voice. It seemed the beast was not so easily discouraged. And it was charging directly toward our boat, on the surface. That it intended to use that mouthful of pointed teeth this time, I had no doubts. I could see at least three spears protruding from its dark humped back. What use would my spear be against such a monster?

It does not swim very fast, a part of me was thinking at the same time. The itzo was not made for speed, with great oar-like flippers propelling it, at least not speed for more than short bursts. It might be able to launch itself quickly from the depths with a few powerful strokes.

Spears were again hurled, but I knew that I was not accurate enough in my throws to hit it in a vulnerable spot save by chance. So I held mine and waited. On it came, lifting its head, jaws agape, at the last moment, and fell upon our boat. I aimed my spear at that great saucer-like eye, glaring less than a meter from me, driving it in with all the force I had.

The itzo rolled, shattering what remained of the craft and throwing us all into the frigid saltwater. Had it been hurt? Had my spear or any spear been effective? I began to paddle quickly to another boat. I knew how to swim; some of my comrades apparently didn't. I grabbed one thrashing man by his beard and dragged him along. It was fortunate that he did not panic and fight me; it was fortunate too that the waves, though large, were smooth rollers. In rough water, none of us might have survived.

Mazi was helping one crewman to a different boat. That was good. Where was the other? Reaching arms helped me and the man I towed climb aboard. I hoped that was the last boat we were to lose!

When I found my feet I also found the entire crew staring soundlessly across the water. There floated the carcass of the itzo, still twitching but obviously mortally wounded.

TSAR OF THE EMPTY LANDS

"That should feed us for a while," was all I could say.

21. Poems

"I thought at first it was some sort of ancient whale, perhaps something akin to the orca," said Konosi, surveying the body of the itzo, stretched out on the beach. "But I see now it is one of the great swimming reptiles of the far past." The carcass was about twelve meters long, with the head fully a quarter of that. I had thought it larger when it was attacking, not that it wasn't quite big enough as was.

Already, work had begun on butchering it. "There is not so much fat on these," remarked one of men, peeling back the leathery hide with a flint knife. "Not like a whale at all." Though they all knew of the itzo and some had spied one, none had ever heard of killing one and bringing it to shore.

Mazi was examining it, stepping off its length, peering into the great toothy maw. "The itzo likes to lurk in the deep water of bays and fjords and ambush those creatures that pass above. So have I always heard." He pondered the wounds, counting them, pushing the haft of a spear in to check their depth. "Who can say which thrust killed it? All of them, maybe. Your spear in the eye is as likely as any, Yuzi, if it went to the brain." Further butchering might reveal that, not that it mattered greatly.

We had lost only one man. That is one too many, of course, but better than might have been expected. Another had broken ribs.

"Is this the most dangerous inhabitant of the waters?" I asked.

There was divided opinion on this. Some named a creature that was surely the giant squid. There was mention of a large predatory seal of some sort, and of the orca. "Stay with us and you will meet all of them!" I was told.

I was not tempted; already I had decided to return inland, even before the hunt. This was not my place nor these my people. "I will go back with the group that leaves tomorrow," I announced. I think Mazi was disappointed.

"I'll be with you," said Daniel. That didn't seem to bother anyone. More than half of those who had made the journey chose to go back to the village. That, I think, was expected by most. Konosi chose to stay here by the bay. Of that, Mazi did approve.

I thought I might miss his thoughts on things. But I no longer needed a council to advise me. For now, I was only another man of this village to which we were returning. We carried as much dried meat and fish and skins as we could bear on our trip back. Other useful goods too, bone and ivory, even shells. All these we bore on our backs. No wagon nor even a travois would have been able to pass over the rocky barren terrain, even had we such.

Some sort of litter might have helped. I would think on that when we got to the village. It seemed there would be much time to think on many things through the cold dark months to come. Already we were entering autumn. One could see and feel the difference. The sun was lower in the sky, and set sooner. There was a chill in the air, but less rain.

Mazi did not return with us. Another man, who had come to the bay later than we, served as our guide. He was one of the elders, a lean and leathery middle-aged man named Veti. I could call many of the people here 'lean and leathery,' I suppose. This land made its inhabitants so.

It was making me so too, I imagined, but there were no mirrors here. There was no time to think of things like that in our first weeks here, when we were focused on our survival, but now it seemed odd not to be able to see ones image. There were many things of that sort one missed, at least at times.

Reading, for one. No written word here in our empty land. There was art; I had seen surprisingly realistic images scratched into bits of ivory or reindeer antler. And there was poetry, or perhaps I should say song. The two ever went together. The man who led us today, Veti, often broke into long tuneless song-poems about some subject or another. My grasp of the language was not yet all it could be.

"I am not prepared to try my hand at poetry in our new tongue," Daniel confided. "Yet it seems pointless to compose anything in Russian."

"But you are Russian," I pointed out, "and always will be, no matter how long you dwell here." And if he or I or anyone else decided to move on in search of another home, would we still speak the words we were now learning?

"You are a bard?" asked Veti. We made it a point to always speak in our new language, to practice it, to make it our own. Also, it was more polite.

"I was," Daniel admitted. "So was Yuzi."

"Ah, you must give us something to pass our time," said our guide. "It is wearisome otherwise."

"I shall try to come up with something if Yuzi will," replied Daniel.

"But I already have," I admitted and at once regretted. Both men looked at me expectantly. "Only a few foolish verses."

"All poets are fools," spoke Veti, smiling.

"Yes," agreed Daniel. "Share with your fellow fools."

Ah, why not? "This came from a remark Leni made about trolls," I told them, and began:

Trolls eat anything, including each other;
maybe their sister — perhaps not Mother.
You may find small bits of someone you know
stuck in their beards that wag to and fro.
Those beards they are long, those beards they are green;
they're never combed out nor are they kept clean.
Trolls deny nothing to their appetite;
pray you don't run into one in the night!
So now you are warned, if a troll be your friend,
he just might eat you as well, in the end.

"Best not let any of our troll friends hear that," felt Daniel.

"Oh, they would think it is funny," said Veti. "Trolls are odd. It sounds like the sort of poem they make up themselves." Then he repeated it, word for word. In a non-literate society, memory tends to be well-developed. "It needs a tune," he decided. "Any of the old ones would do." He tried out several as we marched on.

"Your work has not changed so much, even in a different language," Daniel said later. "You avoid trying to seem serious."

"It is safer so," I reminded him.

22. Berries

The shaman's home was a warren of the half-buried houses these people built, connected by short and narrow passages, but each opening as well to the outer air. Vasa shared one of these chambers with other young unmarried women and girls, granddaughters of Ati. I was never quite sure how many of them there were. We sat now in his main house, the largest of the rooms.

"It is fortunate she is still young," Ati told me. "Many do not come into their gift until they are her age." I still had considerable skepticism when it came to that gift. But the girl seemed to be doing well under the old shaman's tutelage.

"I was haunted by vague images back in our world," she whispered. "Little more than the shadows of hidden things. Here I can see them more clearly."

Ati nodded in approval. "You have grown but there is much yet to learn." She nodded, rather eagerly. Vasa was enjoying her lessons, it seemed. "But now," he continued, "it is more important you go help gather the berries."

Almost everyone in the village was engaged in this, while the fruit was ripe and hanging thick and purplish on the bushes. I think they were a sort of blueberry. Even the hunters and woodcutters had come down out of the hills to take part.

There were bears to compete with the pickers but they were small and shy ones, nothing like the behemoth we had killed on the beach. The foxes and birds liked the berries too. I did not begrudge them a few but we needed to ensure our own survival.

Vasa and I joined a party that sought berries north and west of the village. "There will soon be reindeer here," I was told. "The herds are headed north and will cross over the hills to their winter pastures."

"Wolves will follow," I also heard. I had seen no wolves but had seen skins so I could certainly believe in them. We slept in a small village of earthen houses the first night, not returning home. Most chose to sleep outside.

Few occupied those houses right then for they were used by the herders through the winter. While in the south, in the summer pastures, those who tended the reindeer slept mainly in the open or in tents. I lay awake that night, looking to the skies, clear and thick with stars. These were perhaps the last warm nights of the year, an almost-summer briefly returned.

I could see Vasa sitting up, also gazing at the heavens. Had she taken a lover or pledged herself to any man? I was ignorant of the marriage customs here aside from the fact that they existed. Learning them had not been a priority. I sat up myself.

The girl slipped over to sit beside me. "It is a strange and beautiful land," I said to her.

"It feels like — like home," came her near-whisper of a reply. "As if I were meant to be in this place." I could say nothing of the same sort and so kept my silence. But I could not say it was worse than the Russia I had left behind.

"So you will find a husband and stay here?"

Vasa did not answer for a time. "Ati would love for me to marry his grandson." There was her endearing giggle again. "Any grandson! He believes there is a fair chance that a child would have shamanic abilities."

"Ah. And do any of them take your fancy?"

"They are all, um, nice enough. Nice enough to have around occasionally when they aren't off herding reindeer or hunting." I could tell her tone was not quite serious. "I would be an important person, of course, the shaman of the tribe, and they wouldn't dare cross me in anything."

I was the one to laugh now, and Vasa joined me. I put an arm around her, not thinking of anything but friendship and the sharing of mirth. A moment later, our lips met.

We had both been working our way toward this without admitting it, hadn't we? There in the shadows of the rounded and weathered volcanic hills of the north lands, Vasilina and I made love.

"You will have to have a house of your own where I can visit you," she whispered later, as we lay entangled beneath our seal skin. "I should remain with Ati."

"And all his grandsons?" I asked.

"Jealous already? Surely you did not think you were enough to satisfy me, Tsar Josef!" She dissolved into further giggles.

"Let's find out," I suggested and pulled her to me.

In the gray of just before dawn, I felt her rise and wrap herself in our cover. "I must go clean myself up," she murmured. There was a spring and stream nearby. That was why the village was where it was.

I could probably stand to bathe myself too. I would follow in a little while. Give her privacy now. I had suspected, but now known, that Vasa was a virgin. Yes, give her a little time.

Time was perhaps all we had in this world. In these empty lands.

23. Opasis

The autumn equinox was an important event in the lives of those who dwelt in the empty lands. The equinoxes very much marked the changes of the seasons. Summer and winter were all that mattered here, the two halves of life. The solstices didn't mean much.

There would be a gathering of priests from all around at some sort of sacred shrine. I had been hearing of this for some time. But life went on for the people of the village, the dawn to dusk preparation for the winds of winter to come. No time of year was busier, I was assured.

There was still hunting. That would continue to taper off, but some would go out and hunt through the winter. "Sitting in a house all through the cold times is too boring," I was told. They would not go into the high mountains, of course. That would be impossible.

These people knew the bow but used it little. It was less suitable to their needs than the spear, and the proper materials to craft bows and arrows were scarce. It seemed those who lived further north, those herders of sheep they had mentioned, used bows, composite bows made of horn.

The reindeer were being brought across the hills, herd by herd. Leni said hello to us, spent a night with his wife, and then was gone again. The wife was busy preparing for the festival anyway.

Vasa and I were a couple now and all knew it. Yet she lived with Ati still. The old shaman was disdainful of the priests and their ceremonies. "Charlatans," sniffed Ati. "Their visions are no more than hallucinations caused by the herbs they take." I again sat in his house. I was a regular visitor.

"But they believe in them, Father," one of his daughters reminded him. "As do the people."

Vasa hesitated before saying, "Maybe the gods do speak to them."

Ati stared at her from beneath his white brows. "Gods? I am not even sure they exist!"

"But they come and talk with me sometimes, when I send myself questing."

The shaman could only stare some more. I had no opinion on any of this and hoped I never would.

Opasis they named the festival of the equinox. The main celebration was held in the hills, the divide between north and south. Anyone could see the symbolism in that. Those who could not travel there held their own rites wherever they might. There was no reason Vasa and I should not go, though it was a journey of two days.

People came from all over and, of course, their priests as well. These priests seemed more pantheistic or even animistic than aught else, though they would name off some god or another from time to time. There were many small villages or solitary houses from which women and men came, even some along the south side of the hills that remained inhabited through the winter. Konosi and others came from the sea. I had never mentioned to the people here that he was a priest nor, I think, had he. Not that it could be kept secret; all who had come from the other world knew it.

He would have fit right in. They were a grave bunch, both men and women, and very much full of themselves at this time of year. I suspect they were fairly normal the rest of the time, and did the same work as everyone else. This land could not support a caste of full-time priests.

Perhaps some of their gravity was due to the herbs they had ingested. These made them rather glassy-eyed as well. Ask me not what they were. Vasa might have known. I think some of the ordinary folk knew too and indulged in their use.

I would rather have ingested alcohol myself. There was none in this land. It was not something I had thought of much but I missed it at that moment. What good is a festival without at least a little beer? Probably those berries we had gathered could have been turned into wine. Alas, they were all dried into raisins now. This must be a project for the new year, I decided — either learn to make alcohol or go someplace they had it!

Konosi found us after we had all arrived, in a pleasant enough — though typically barren — little valley, cupped in the hills. "I understand you are together now," he said. "If you wish a marriage in the Orthodox faith, you need only ask me." I do not think he considered it overly important and did not again mention the idea. Nor did Vasa.

The tall man turned his eyes toward the group of priests, performing some baffling ceremony of their own, involving the shaking of rattles and the throwing down of handfuls of small bones on the ground. An augury, I think. "They have a litany of gods and goddesses, most of them nothing more than names. Deities that have been brought by each nationality that has come through the path we followed."

"Including Jesus?" I asked.

"I would not be surprised." He smiled slyly. "Perhaps we should introduce the great god Marx to them."

"They worship him already, without knowing his name." They were better socialists than those we had left behind.

A small group of trolls sat to one side, observing without a great deal of interest. I think maybe they came for the herbs too. "I wonder what sort of gods they worship," I whispered, nodding in their direction. Was there a great Father Troll in the sky?

"I am told trolls are all atheists. But I am also told they are ancestor worshipers." Konosi shrugged. "I suppose the two are not mutually exclusive."

Olga had put on her reindeer antlers and cape. That was Leni's wife, our village priestess. "She serves Benesi," said Vasa.

Benesi — that sounded familiar. "A name from our own Slavic mythology, I think." Changed some over time in this land.

Konosi nodded. "You may be right. The antlered trickster of our ancestors."

Vasa's face held something akin to a pout. "I have not yet been able to speak to Benesi. The gods do not pay much attention to any of us."

"The gods exist?" Konosi's attempt to sound amused could not cover a tinge of sarcasm.

"Ati and the shamans have taught me that all things exist somewhere," she stated, as if explaining the idea to a child. "Therefor, so do the gods."

Konosi did not deign to offer a rebuttal. He did not take Vasa at all seriously. But I had heard something I did not understand. "Shamans? When have you met other shamans?"

"Oh, I speak to them from afar. It is one of the skills Ati has taught me." I chose not to question further also.

But Vasa chose to tease me. "Benesi is the true Lord of the Empty Lands, Tsar Josef," she said. "He rules over all wild things." She giggled. "And can turn into a bear!"

"Then he had best not visit when I have my rifle with me," was the only answer I had to that.

The whole affair continued into the night, with much slow and monotonous singing, intended as a farewell-and-hurry-back to the Sun Boat.

Maybe it sounded better to those who took the proper herbs.

24. A Hunt

There was to be one last organized hunt, and I intended to be with it. First, I joined those who transported food to the high caves of the hills for storage. Men would need visit them through the winter to bring supplies back to the villages. It was too cold there for men to stay and guard them but the trolls kept a watch — and took a small share for themselves. That was an unspoken agreement that worked well for all.

Already it was bitterly cold in the heights. Even in summer it was quite cool; my guess is the yogurt I had eaten had come from milk kept here, deep in the caves where there was always ice. In truth, it was more a place for summer storage than winter; when the cold truly came to the empty lands, food could be kept fresh anywhere!

We did not return to the village and the lowlands but continued deeper into the hills for the hunt. This was higher and further west than I had before gone here; indeed, we were on the porches of the great mountains themselves.

"Some go higher in the summer," I was told. "Some go all the way across."

"What lies there?" I asked. I would have been no more than casually curious not long ago. Now that I was thinking more and more of moving on in the spring, I felt I should know all I could.

"The land on the other side of the mountains," was the answer. Well, at least there was one. I would have to seek out another for information — or maybe go myself.

We hunted anything. Taking larger animals was more efficient, to be sure, but rabbits could feed us as we continued our hunt. There were trees up here, hardy twisted conifers clinging to the rocky soil. Surprisingly little snow lay on that soil.

Some days we took the wild goats that climbed along the cliff faces, spearing them when they strayed too close, or knocking them from their perches with thrown rocks. Then we had to climb far down to find their bodies. Spears were better. There were large deer, too, larger than the reindeer, with spreading sharp-tined antlers. These we found in the valleys; already they were moving down from the highlands and would be close enough to the villages to hunt through the winter.

Above, strange shapes in the sky. Some were great birds, I could tell, condors perhaps, or eagles. Others I was not so certain of — and I could recognize what Leni had offhandedly named a dragon, a long thin body and wings not at all bird-like. Those never came close enough for me to tell what sort of beast they truly were. That might have been just as well.

All we caught, we butchered, and the meat we cached in the cold places the men knew. The skins too we kept and as much else as was practical. There were uses for almost all parts of an animal. "We will leave some of this in the caves," our leader explained to me. "You do not have to carry it all the way back." From time to time, a pair of us traveled to those caves, each burdened with what we had taken from two or three large game animals.

The second time I did this, there were trolls inside. Friendlies, I assumed, though I was on my guard. "Yuzi!" one called to me in greeting. Mug? It must be. I could barely speak a few words to the little troll-man the last I had seen him. Now we could converse.

"Wife," he said, directing a thumb toward a troll woman behind him. He made no further introduction. She was fully as tall as Mug, and built much the same. No beard, however. His wife was busy picking through the stored foodstuffs and paid me no attention. A handful of other trolls, of both genders were doing the same. Troll children, too, and one woman had a troll baby nursing at her breast. All wore loincloths and no more.

"You might as well look at this too," I said, depositing my load on the rock floor.

"Fresh meat is always better," Mug replied, beckoning the others to come. He looked up at me and gave me a troll wink. "Even if trolls will eat anything."

"As long as they don't eat too much of it," said my companion, laying down his load of meat.

"You know we take only a little now and then," said Mug. He sounded almost hurt but his face suggested very much otherwise. "We chased away some goblins who were nosing about here. They would have grabbed it all."

"We thank you," I said. Goblins? I didn't want to ask.

Trolls were quite strange enough. But it did not really feel so odd now to share a meal and a cave with them. Their strange songs do not seem so strange after a time.

But one has not lived until he has seen troll women dance.

25. Winter Comes

The first winter storm came howling into the empty lands, and life changed. There was not so much snow but all assured me it would accumulate through the months to come.

The predominant winds seemed to sweep in from the south and southwest. The hills and mountains did protect us some here. Perhaps the village was in the best spot on the whole of the island. But it seemed to be a very large island so I only guessed this.

How large? I said I could only guess, didn't I? Much larger that the Iceland which it resembled, that was certain. Perhaps in the spring I could find out.

People stayed snug in their houses, burning little stone lamps filled with the fat of seals or whales, or oil from the livers of fish, and worked on what could be worked on. There was much done with leather, and with other useful parts of animals. There was also little privacy, or more of my hours would have been filled by Vasa.

Vasa — Ati claimed that she already was surpassing him in the skills of shamanry. The mystical side of those skills, that is; he considered the girl still woefully insufficient in the use of herbs and the ways of healing. "She is more sorceress than shaman," he confided. "Vasa was born more powerful than any I have known."

I did not know what to make of any of this. Was all of it delusion on their parts? I was surprised to find Daniel now more willing to believe than I was. "If we are to believe we have come to a different world, a different universe, perhaps, why can we not also believe this?" he argued. "Are sorcerers any more impossible than trolls?" But I had seen trolls, fought trolls, shared meals with trolls. Sorcery was not a physical reality.

He and I spent much time together. Yes, we shared the same house so that was unavoidable but we also worked together, attempting to learn the crafts of our adopted people. Daniel may have been better with his hands than I, but his eyesight hampered him — all the more so by the light of a flickering oil lamp.

And he had rediscovered his poetry. Not Russian poetry but poetry in his new tongue. I could find no name for the language we spoke other than a word that meant just 'language,' more or less. Maybe 'words' would be more accurate.

I did not have much in the way of words myself. I felt used up in that winter, living only the moments I could spend with Vasa. Daniel discreetly visited friends from time to time so we might have those moments. It seemed there was never any occasion for me to reciprocate; he had managed to alienate most of the available women by that time.

"We must find him a wife to take him in hand," said Leni, on one of his visits. These were not infrequent, for the reindeer herds were close by and so was his wife. "My daughters are too young." He sounded quite emphatic about that. I was not sure how early they married here. It might have just been an excuse not to have Daniel in the family.

"There are still far more men than women here," I reminded him. Even with some of my people relocated to other villages, this was so. "I think there is too much competition for him."

"He brings it on himself. Danayeli has rejected good women." Danayeli was what some called him. It had not been universally adopted and Daniel did not seem to care one way or another.

I agreed that this was true. "Also, he is not certain he will remain here, come spring," I said. Nor was I, but this I did not say.

Leni nodded gravely, his eyes of the floor. "Yes, I would expect some of the men to seek new lands. Some of the women too, maybe." Then he looked up at me, smiling. "It is good we both have women with a place here!"

Ah, there it was. Could I be as Leni? Vasa did indeed have a place here, if she wished it. She sometimes seemed as restless as I. But we could wed and remain, Vasa the shaman to these people, I perhaps a hunter. It could be a life. It could even be a good life.

Twenty years from now, Yuzi would sit with the other village elders, guiding his people. There would be children, many children, and grandchildren. And he would ever wonder what lay beyond that horizon he had not chosen to cross.

It was yet winter. There would be much time to think on these things.

26. Elders

The elders did not sit outside much at this time of year, though there were sometimes fine days. Do not think we were closed in our little houses all the time!

Anna sat with them still, and she and her counsel were welcome. It was recognized that Anton was her husband — Olga even performed some ceremony for them to make it official. I think Anna was making sure no other woman got ideas.

Anton, the old poacher that he was, had quickly integrated with those who hunted. Tani he had come to be called. He was gone almost as much, therefor, as Leni. Anna did not greatly mind. She had other concerns for she made all things her concerns. I know not if she had any skills other than scheming and talking but she did those well.

No longer was she my secret police for I was no longer at the center of power. Indeed, she paid no great attention to me anymore. Vasa thought that funny. Apparently, so did Olga.

"The priestess has become my friend," Vasa told me. We had my house to ourselves that afternoon and had been making the most of it. Still, one must sometimes rest and that rest may be filled with talk. "Ati does not completely approve. He feels it upsets the balance of power."

I pushed back the fur cover — it was the skin of the bear I had slain so long ago, carried all the way here on our journey. Learning I had killed that bear definitely boosted my reputation here. "The lamp needs adjusted," I muttered, attempting to get the wick where it should be without burning my fingers. "So," I said, turning to the girl, "Olga dislikes our Anna?"

Vasa furrowed up her narrow forehead. "I don't know," she admitted. "She is amused by her, um — machinations." The last word was in Russian as she could not think of a proper one in our new language. Neither could I. Our talk often mingled the two tongues. Maybe we were creating a new pidgin.

"Anna will scheme even if there is no reason," I said, slipping back under the bear skin. The lamp shone a little brighter, a little more steady.

Not much.

"No one needs to scheme here," whispered Vasa. "There is no use for power."

That was perhaps a tad naïve but I understood her point. People will still compete for prestige, if nothing else. And for mates — that was always there. But who would desire to rule over a handful of hunters and herders?

Ah, Anna, of course. It was just her nature. She had once ruled over a handful of whores. "Those who feel they have no worth themselves," I whispered back, "make up for it by seeking power over others."

"You are wise, my tsar," Vasa breathed, and kissed me. It did sound wise, did it not? I had no idea whether it was true. "And now," she went on, "I must assert my power over you."

"I am a conquered nation," I told her. And maybe that *was* true.

It was sometime later that Olga suggested a marriage ceremony for Vasa and me. Maybe Leni suggested it, maybe she decided it on her own. "In the spring, if you wish to wait," she said. "The feast of the equinox is a popular time for such things." I nodded agreeably. That was some time off and much could happen before then. "But," she continued, her voice a little lower, as if confiding a secret, "if you were wed now I suspect we could shuffle people about and find you a house of your own." That was certainly a nice little piece of enticement.

And why should we not marry? Oh, yes, all those things I have already said, all those thoughts I have already had. "She needs to study longer with Ati," was the reply — the excuse? — I made. "Perhaps spring. Vasa and I must talk on it."

"Do not talk too long," the priestess warned. "Ati has too many grandsons. They would not take time for talk at all."

Olga was persuasive. And spring was still far away. To have Vasa now, for her to be mine and I to be hers — might that not be better? "Tell me," I asked her, "how long did Leni court you?"

"He did need to learn the language first," she admitted, and then smiled broadly. "But he also did accept as soon as I proposed."

Of course he did. Of course. Leni knew what was good for him.

27. Gods and Wizards

"He is far away but he is coming," pronounced Vasa.

"The one you saw before?" I could not remember the name she had given.

"Yes, Hurasu." She gave a quick sidelong glance to Ati, who sat impassively. "In the spring. I think."

"That would be sensible," spoke the old shaman. "Hurasu has never spoken to me but I have heard of him. He is the greatest of all sorcerers in this world."

Vasa had known the name before ever meeting Ati. Was Hurasu real? Or was Ati just playing along somehow, keeping up a pretense of magical power? I found it hard to believe he was such a charlatan.

"But there are others," she said, rather quietly. "And not all live in this world."

A brief break in the shaman's composure, quickly controlled. "It is not wise to seek into the other worlds. There are beings there too powerful, too dangerous, for human minds." He seemed concerned but perhaps did not want to sound as if he was exaggerating the hazard. "So have shamans ever been warned."

"Gods." I am not sure why I said that, except that Vasa had once mentioned them. Ati had surely never gone seeking them. Maybe he did not have the ability.

The ability. Did I now believe in this?

"Some gods seem quite nice," objected Vasa. "Mostly ones the people here don't know. I think maybe they are bored and are willing to chat." She laughed. "They seem able to learn my language almost instantly. The wizards can't do that. Not even Hurasu."

I had to smile at the idea of this thin little girl passing the time with deities. "Immortality would be boring, I think."

So was winter. We were at least two months past the equinox now. I did not keep close track of the days. Olga would know. It was the darkest time of the year, day being a few hours of a wan sun, lying low in the sky. Nights were long and cold and the winds of winter howled around our houses. Visiting, sitting and talking, was one way to relieve that boredom, and Ati always seemed pleased to see me.

"Then you and Hurasu did not speak in words," said the shaman.

"That is so," agreed Vasa. "He seemed to want to keep a distance for now. I know not why."

"He is sensible," stated Ati. "You should learn from his example." We both had to laugh at his earnestness and, shortly, the old man was chuckling too.

"It is sensible, too," he said, "not to sit and talk all the day. Or is it night? Go help my granddaughters prepare the meal, will you my girl? I would say a few more word to Yuzi before pushing him out into the cold."

She disappeared through one of the short, low, stone-lined passageways connecting the houses. Ati watched and then turned to me. "Vasa has gone places she is not willing to admit to me. Maybe she would to you, if you knew the right questions."

"She is in danger?"

"Maybe." He reconsidered that. "Not maybe. It is always dangerous, some. That is part of being a shaman." I could only nod and let him go on.

"Even I can sense that there is another powerful sorcerer whispering to her. Not Hurasu." He appeared both worried and puzzled. "Vasa may not even know he is there. It was this sort of thing against which I warned her."

"But he is a wizard, as this Hurasu."

"I am not sure. What I feel of his presence is very strange. Distant. I think he may not be in this world at all, yet he somehow has a bond to it."

I thought on this for a few moments. "Would Hurasu be aware of him too?"

The old man spread his arms. "I would think so. It might be why he comes. Or a part of why he comes."

There was nothing to say but, "I suppose we shall learn in the spring."

Ati cocked an eyebrow at me. "Much may be learned in the spring. You are also a presence in Vasa's life. Will that continue?"

"Will we wed? I do not know. I do not even know if I will still be here when winter comes again."

"Ah." I thought he would say no more for a few seconds. "Perhaps it is but a winter romance. Such happen when the darkness surrounds our little houses, but they fade before the returning sunlight."

Maybe they did. Maybe Vasa would wed one of his grandsons instead. Who could see? Who could know? I made my goodbye to the old shaman and went out into the darkness.

28. The Longest Night

The folk here did not celebrate the solstice as they did the equinox, but they knew when it came. I had become restless and was at the village by the sea when it came. It seemed a good place to think.

"Perhaps Father Christmas will visit," I joked with Konosi. Did he know of Father Christmas? I had read many English authors — too many, maybe — but his education might have been quite different.

"I fear Saint Nicholas could not find his way here," he said, "nor is there a star to guide the Three Kings." The priest gazed out over the dark wild waters, doing battle with an icy wind. "I have never felt so alone before in this land."

"You have always had your faith before," I said. I knew it had sustained him, both here and in Russia.

The man sighed deeply. "Do you believe in God, Yuzi?"

I answered carefully. "I believe in a god in the broadest sense." We stood unspeaking for a few seconds, looking out over the sea, before I went on. "If anything, coming here has made me more of a believer. In a god, that is. It makes Christianity even more questionable."

"I have felt something of the same," he admitted. "Maybe being a Christian belongs to the world we left behind. There is no Church here, no Patriarch. But there is still a God."

I said nothing of the varied gods Vasa claimed to have encountered. That would muddy up the water again. "But I remain a priest," he continued. "It is my calling." He turned to look at me with his dark grave eyes. "As it is yours to lead."

"There are none to follow either of us," came my retort, perhaps more harshly than was needed.

"That will change if you decide to move north in the spring. You will be hetman again. No other could be chosen."

He was probably right. Leaving these lands was not something I thought much of right then. It seemed wearisome and pointless at times. Why trek off somewhere else when I had found a home here? Of course, Vasa stood in the middle of all the arguments for staying.

"Would you, too, leave?" I asked of him.

"I might," he admitted. "Maybe by boat. Or at least explore the coasts to the north."

"Ah, but are those fjords not where the itzo lurk in wait?" I said this jokingly.

He laughed. "An inconvenience! Let us get inside." It was near pitch-black now, on this, the longest of nights. The skies were clearing and stars shone through here and there.

We crawled into the largest of the common houses. Many bachelors lived here and shared these; the relatively few couples had smaller houses. I think there might have been one unmarried woman there; I do not know where she slept but the bachelors undoubtedly did.

None were asleep now. They huddled around a puny fire of driftwood. The smoke circled about the room and escaped through a small hole in the ceiling. That would be shut up later. There was no need to keep a fire going in here with all these bodies to warm the space.

"Konosi!" someone called. "Konosi is a priest."

"Of which god?" asked someone else.

"It doesn't matter. One's as good as another." There were grunts of agreement to this.

"Give us a rite of the longest night!"

"Yes, yes," came a clamor. "It is when the Sun Boat turns around," I heard, and, "The Christ child is born." There were a few of our own people, Russians, among the group, and not all of them had subscribed to official Marxist atheism.

Konosi took a seat in their circle, sitting erect. "I do not know all the gods of this land," he began, his voice become firmer and more sonorous as he continued, "but I know this was the night the Great Father sent his son to live among men." There were murmurs. The Father was one of their gods, the god of the skies. "As he was born on this night, so are all we, so is all the land, reborn."

That didn't seem to stray too far from Christian doctrine, I thought. "In my homeland there are many rites celebrated. Again, I do not know your ways." He gave them a warm smile. "It was customary to eat fish on this night." Laughs all around; that was about all they did eat. "And feasting tomorrow — in the middle of winter we mark the return to abundance, the spring and summer that will surely come." He looked around the room. "The birth of our world."

It was a perfect little sermon for this group. But they probably still expected some sort of ceremony. That was what priests did.

"In the land from which I came," Konosi said, "we sometimes brought green branches or even trees into our houses to mark this day. To remember that summer does return and will return."

"This is done by our people," came a voice. "There would be pine boughs gathered in the other villages but none are near here."

"Ah. Then I guess feasting tomorrow will have to be good enough."

I spoke up. I am not sure why. "What of a yule log?" This was another tradition that might be outside his personal experience, but the priest surely knew of it.

He nodded. "Yes, we would burn a fire through the longest night, to show we are aware that darkness does not last nor win." Konosi stared at the little fire. "I think a lamp burning would be as good." He took one of oil lamps and lit it from the embers. He made a show of it, moving slowly and with a bit of exaggeration.

And that was all. The men seemed satisfied with his impromptu rite. Konosi seemed satisfied too. "Yes," I whispered to him later, "it is your calling."

"More than a calling, I see now," he replied, his voice low and measured. "All this reminded me of that fact. I am as a lover. My faith is a passion." Konosi remained silent for the better part of a minute. "You avoid passion," he said.

"I do?" I knew better than to deny it but neither was I going to admit to this.

"That is not a bad thing in one who leads. But do not let it make the rest of your life empty." Konosi spread his arms wide, attracting a few disinterested glances from our drowsy companions. "As empty as these lands."

I had no answer. We both slept through the remainder of the longest night, Konosi's lamp flickering softly in the dark.

29. Herds

These were the leanest times, as winter slowly relaxed its grip on the empty lands but it was not yet possible to replenish our stocks of food. Oh, there was hunting and there were the reindeer herds. Those helped. Most of what we ate had been stored away and if that were gone, we would starve, unless we chose to deplete the herds. That could cause us to starve later on. It was a precarious existence here.

Some should certainly leave. North? Everyone said that was the way. To the south, life was even harder. Across the mountains? Most had only heard evil of that land. Considering the prevailing winds, I suspected it would be less hospitable than our side of the island. There would be more snow.

Not so much snow fell here but it did, as promised, accumulate. Winter was a dry season, relatively. The reindeer were able to paw through it and feed in their northern pastures. I spent time with the herders. I felt I should learn all the tasks of this life.

I also sensed that it was expected that all men should know something of herding. It was the most central part of their life. I might even help drive the reindeer back across the hills when the time came. Not so far away was that. Six weeks maybe.

Much could happen in six weeks. Herding was cold work, it was tedious work, but it was not very hard work. I remained bundled in my sealskin parka and pants, my mittens and boots, most of the time. We would patrol the edge of the herd, make sure no reindeer went astray, keep an eye open for predators. There were indeed wolves, as I had been told, and I suspect they would just as readily have grabbed a man as a deer. We were armed with spears and always worked in pairs. That was as much to prevent us from getting lost as for protection.

My mind would go to Vasa. I would much rather be with her than these homely four-legged creatures and their equally homely two-legged guardians. But my being here allowed another man to be with his woman, if he had one, or at least be in the comfort and companionship of the villages. I missed the girl. Did I love her? Konosi was right about passion. I was not passionate about Vasa. This I had known from the start. It did not mean I did not love her. I would ache if I lost her.

The day was bright, the sun shining across the snow. The sun sat higher in the skies now, stayed with us a little longer each day. There would still be storms. There would still be more cold and snow; we would not deceive ourselves there. A shadow moved across the terrain, blue against the white hills. An eagle? A reindeer was too large for them to take.

I pointed and my fellow herder looked up. "Dragon. It might go after one of our deer."

From what I had heard, dragons tended to go for smaller prey too. They could be a problem, it seemed, when the calves were born. That would be a while yet, after the herds had moved south, and most within a few days of each other. But when a creature is hungry enough, it might change its hunting habits.

I had not seen a dragon from nearly so close before. It was not really very large, in terms of mass, all wings and long thin body. There was fur on that body. I had expected scales, of course. This was no reptile. It swooped in for a look at us and then climbed away, the bat-like wings carrying it up till its shape was no longer recognizable. But we knew what it was.

"It will either dive or decide on some other prey," said my companion. "We can't really stop its attack but it will be vulnerable on the ground."

I doubted the beast could get aloft with a full-grown reindeer. It must feed where it killed, or carry parts away. Ha, I shouldn't assume it would only attack the deer. It might find humans tasty! The herd seemed to have sensed it and were milling about.

The dragon neither stooped upon us nor flew elsewhere; rather, it glided down slowly to alight on a hill not too far away. Large ears pricked up as it sat on its haunches, watching us. It looked very thin. "It is starving," I whispered. I know not what possessed me to do what I did next.

Our own supplies were near. A pair of herders always had some, for they might not reunite with their fellows for days. It was also not unusual to slaughter a reindeer on taking up a post, to provide that food supply. I ran to the cache and dug a chunk of meat out of the snow; it was simply the first I came on, a rack of reindeer ribs. These I carried nearly halfway to the dragon, which watched me carefully. As I watched it!

Then I backed away, slowly, cautiously, still keeping my eyes on the beast. It crept forward, a bit ungainly for it must support itself on two legs and two wings. I do not know who came up with the ridiculous idea of dragons with four legs in addition to wings. It makes no sense.

The dragon looked even less reptilian from closer up. The body with its dark brown fur reminded me of a marten. But much, much larger. It settled down on the meat and began tearing pieces loose, trilling occasionally. It was a basso profundo trill. "It will probably come begging for more now," my fellow herder muttered. He looked out at the dragon and laughed. "But I do not begrudge it."

"At least it isn't bothering the herd now," I said. We could afford to lose a little meat but it would be a great inconvenience if the reindeer were scattered. We both recognized this.

The dragon suddenly lifted its head, peered off somewhere to our left. Naturally, we looked. A man was approaching slowly over the hills. The way he moved, his gait, said he wore snow shoes. Those were a hindrance in our herding work and rarely truly needed, but were useful when traveling longer distances.

"It is Leni," I said, and waved toward him.

His voice came echoing over the snow. "Vasa is hurt. You must return to the village."

30. Vasa

It was not a physical injury. This much I learned from Leni as we traveled. Beyond that, he knew nothing. "Ati watches over her," he said.

To Ati's house I went as soon as we arrived. Vasa was in his own chamber, wrapped in sleeping furs. She opened her eyes, smiled and murmured a greeting, and fell asleep again.

Ati watched her for a moment, then shook his head. "She rests. She heals, I think."

"How did this happen?" I whispered.

"I tried to direct her visions," he said. I took a seat beside him, both facing the small peat fire. "Or to share in them. It comes to the same thing, maybe." One of his daughters came in, carrying food. Ati took only the yogurt. "I hoped to keep her safe."

"From that other you had sensed," I said. He nodded. I knew he would go on when ready.

"I do not truly understand how the gift of shamans works," he told me. "None of us do. Maybe the great sorcerers do. We — send ourselves to other worlds. Some say it is our soul, some say it is part of our physical being. Again, I do not know."

It probably didn't matter either. I nodded politely.

"Mostly those other worlds are safe little places where we may talk to one another from afar." I found that interesting and did not conceal it. "Yes, that is how it works. It is not so complicated. So did Vasa speak even with the great sorcerer who comes."

"Hurasu," I said. "He is still on his way?"

"So it seems. I saw him briefly through her eyes." He sighed of a sudden. "I saw many wonderful things through her eyes. Such power she has, to reach into places undreamed of by one such as I!"

I am sure I frowned. "But dangerous, no?"

"That they are. One could become lost and never return. Ones mind could be blasted by terrible and powerful wizards who dwell in the other worlds." Or gods, I thought, but did not interrupt.

"Vasa knows enough to keep the other worlds at bay, blocked from her thoughts most of the time. This was the first thing I taught her. It is the first thing taught all shamans. Without this knowledge, madness will follow, the voices and visions of the infinite worlds flowing into ones mind."

"We thought Vasa mad at first," I admitted. "Even in our own world, it seems."

"I think it is nearly impossible to see the other worlds in that one from which you came. It would take a great talent to sense them at all." His eyes went again to the slumbering girl. "She went to Hurasu and I went with her. I could not have done it on my own, maybe, and the sorcerer did not object to my presence. And while we were there, another came." He shuddered and sat unspeaking for a long while.

"He came through Vasa, of course, the presence I had dimly sensed before. A great wizard. I think he dwells in another world but am not certain. He seemed both here and elsewhere. It was to challenge Hurasu he came, and Vasa was caught between them."

"Were not you, as well?" I asked. He seemed unharmed.

"No, I was of no interest and linked only to Vasa. I was a bystander, watching through her eyes. In a way." I recognized such things would be hard to put into words. "Hurasu protected her. Had that not been necessary, I believe he might have destroyed the other sorcerer. Or hurt him badly, at least. He made certain that she was able to break free and return." A thin smile. "Taking me with her."

"But she was hurt." That I could see.

"She was. Hurasu spoke to me later, called me and I answered. He made it understood he will hurry to us now, though he has no words in our language. He could not tell me whether the bond that other wizard created with Vasa remains. She should link with no one until he comes."

"Has she tried?" I asked.

"No. Vasa does not seem able to focus long enough for that. I do not know what goes on within her mind, Yuzi. Maybe that other is yet with her. Maybe she wanders lost in other worlds."

"And naught can be done until the sorcerer arrives."

"Who can say? She might heal on her own. Vasa seems to grow stronger." He did not sound overly convinced of this.

"Then I must go to greet this Hurasu and bring him here," I stated.

Part 3. Sorcerers

31. An Expedition

I knew we had covered many hundreds of kilometers between our arrival point and this village. How much further might it be to the northern end of the island? And how would we know when and where this sorcerer would arrive?

Ati had an answer for the second question. "You must have a shaman with you as a guide," he proclaimed. "I have spoken from afar with my brothers and found you one."

That shaman came into the village the next day. He was a troll. With him was our old friend Mug. "I am to keep an eye on this boy," he said, "if you permit us to come along."

I could see no good reason to object, though I tried to think of one. The young troll shaman's name was Vuk, and he was Zup's apprentice. Unlike his master, he could speak the language of the villagers. But he would not speak the language of Hurasu. I had enough understanding of this speaking from afar to know this would be an impediment.

Konosi had also shown up, declaring he would accompany me. Maybe that was just his desire to explore the north but he would be a good man to have along. I did turn down his suggestion that we take one of the skin-covered boats rather than walking.

Our other two — I saw no need for a large group — were men of the empty lands, young hunters both. They were the sort I needed and they were interested in seeing new places. Davati and Misi were they named. I could not see bringing any more of our own people. Not now.

I brought also my rifle. I decided to take only three cartridges, allotting two each to Anton and Ivan. That was all we had and ever would have, we were sure. They would use them if it were necessary.

Snow still covered the ground and would a month more or longer. It was not the best of times to set out. A couple weeks earlier and I would not have attempted it, not even for Vasa. It would have been senseless. Now, we should be alright and the days would grow longer and warmer as we progressed. Maybe there was less snow in the north, too.

Then goodbyes. Daniel was there — Yeli was now the name both the villagers and he accepted — with a girl at his side. One of Olga and Leni's teenage daughters. So much for Leni's disapproval. Leni himself was with the reindeer. We might see him on the way north. Yeli shook my hand and said he was glad he was not going with me.

In the dark of the long dawn, we began our trek north. We passed the first of the herds, moving slowly south, antlered shadows and men who cried out greetings. They might not have known where we were going and I would not take the time to stop and tell them.

We did stop and eat with the herdsmen that evening, giving them our story. None made any comment on it, only nodding their heads. We were doing what we needed to do, as all men must.

I knew the coastline ran north and a little east here. Mazi and others who were of the sea had told me this. Beyond, some said it came back abruptly to the west, but none had ever gone that far. If it were so, best to strike due north or even west of north rather than hugging the edge of the sea. Men had traveled that way, and visited those who lived there, the herders of sheep. But none had gone as far as the water.

We would learn, one way or another. Three more days and we had left the last of the reindeer herds behind us. The land grew gradually less hospitable too, broken and rocky, until there was no pasturage left that would have supported a herd. We hunted sometimes, rather than relying on our stores of dried meat, taking the usual rabbits and once a sort of small shaggy antelope. Konosi thought it might be related to a chamois. That made no difference to the taste.

And each night, Vuk would sit calmly and attempt to speak afar. Of Hurasu he found no sign but it seems he did talk to his master Zup and to Ati. They had no news. Too, he said he had spoken to shamans among the people north of us but they also knew nothing.

You see, I believed in this now. How could I not? Oh, Konosi still had his skepticism but he had not seen what I had. I was grateful that he had chosen to come anyway, even doubting there was an Hurasu.

Did anyone live in this wilderness, an even emptier land than that which we had left? It would be a difficult life, the life of the primitive hunter. No, surely we were alone, our only companions the rock-speared earth and the sky.

32. Goblins

"We are not alone," whispered Misi. Davati nodded an agreement.

"Not men," he said. This time Misi nodded.

"Trolls?" I might need to unsling the Mosin Nagant.

"No," said Vuk. "Goblins. One is trying to speak to me." He stood still for some seconds, oblivious to his surroundings. "Ah," the shaman said at last, "they have heard me trying to reach Hurasu. They know the sorcerer."

"Are they friendly to the sorcerer?" I asked. That made all the difference.

"So it seems," said the troll. "Or they fear his wrath, perhaps. That works just as well." He snickered. "All goblins are sorcerers. None are very good at it. It's just how they are made."

"We might as well move on then," Mug said. "If they wish to show themselves, they will."

We did move on and the goblins did show themselves a little, peeking around distant rocks or from the tops of the steep hills. I could only tell they were small, smaller than the trolls. "Are they, um, a related people?" I asked Mug.

He looked quite offended. Knowing Mug — and trolls in general — by now, I did not take it too seriously. "We are more closely related to you," he stated. "The goblins are of the fay."

"And you are not?" asked Konosi.

I think there was true scorn in Mug's voice this time. "Of course not."

Vuk chortled. "You will see if they come close."

We had to camp eventually. We picked the most defensible spot we could find. But that was as most other evenings.

Eventually, a delegation of the little men did show up, four individuals. Men, I use in the most general sense; they did indeed look less manlike than the trolls. Also, two were female. Wizened little creatures they were, not at all like the barrel-bodied trolls, pale, hairless, and completely naked. Only in their noses did they have a resemblance. They stuck out even further perhaps, but were thin and pointed, not bulbous, with eyes set deep and close on either side.

"One might be their queen," whispered Mug. "You can not be sure unless they tell you."

A male stepped forward and addressed us in a broken pidgin. An interpreter, apparently. "You seek great wizard Urasu?" he asked. "We see 'im coming. On other side water now."

I stepped forward as well. "He will be coming south. We go to escort him on his journey."

The goblins had to talk this over among themselves, in harsh, high-pitched tones. The language sounded nothing like that of the trolls, nor of any humans I have known, for that matter. "Some say we eat you," the interpreter informed us. "Even stinky trolls."

Vuk and Mug seemed to think that was hilarious but kept themselves from laughing outright.

"Neither we nor Hurasu would appreciate that," I told him. I think it puzzled him. Maybe goblins didn't have a sense of humor.

"We not eat," he promised. "You bring Urasu back 'ere?"

"That depends on what the great sorcerer himself decides."

Another goblin conference. I was not sure whether they wanted Hurasu to pass through or not. I *was* sure they were thoroughly afraid of him. "Some remember Urasu. Many years ago," he said. "Thousands. 'E come from south. Like you." He peered at me. "Through gate?"

There was no reason to deny it. "Yes, we two came through the gate." I indicated Konosi with a nod of my head. "Do you mean Hurasu did as well?" Thousands of years? We must be misunderstanding each other.

"It is so, Man. All fay felt 'is coming. Everywhere." The wizened little fellow threw his arms out wide. "We 'oped Urasu would stay on other side of world. But 'e returns." He looked up at me and then at the rest of our party. "Why?"

I did not know. It was not because of Vasa, that was certain. And the rival he had battled seemed to have taken him by surprise. I did suspect his reasons had something to do with the gate. "The great Hurasu does not tell me his reasons," I stated. That would have to do. Maybe best to keep these goblins guessing, too.

Another exchange between the goblins. One female seemed to be the decision maker. "Queen says you may stay," I was informed. "We not bother. Move on tomorrow!"

"Certainly," I replied, "and thank you." I bowed toward the goblin woman. In a moment, all four had disappeared into the gloom.

"Gone to their burrows," said Mug. "A horrible sort of life, really. And yes, Yuzi, they live for thousands of years."

I found I could believe that. But did it also mean the wizard Hurasu was thousands of years old? He could be no human who came from my world.

We set up our cold camp and set sentries as well, despite the goblins' promises. It was not a bad night. I think it was the warmest one I had felt in many months. There was a nearly full moon, disappearing, reappearing through low clouds, silvering the rocky landscape. It was a strange sort of fairyland, but a believable one.

"Are your people long-lived?" I asked Mug as we took our turn at sentry.

"Not like the fay," he replied. "But I may live twice as long as you." After a time, he added. "We trolls do not live as fast as men. We are of the People of the Earth. Our blood runs slower, our bodies cooler."

I had been close to trolls now, walked and worked beside them, taken their hands. I could sense the truth in what he said. But they were more like men than they were different. That too I could tell.

The moon was sinking in the west.

33. Directions

"I think we should head more westerly," was Misi's opinion. "I have heard that is where one will find men."

Davati disagreed this time. "If we continue on this course we will reach the sea. Then we can just follow the coastline."

Neither had ever been anywhere near this far north, of course. They had only heard things. The rest of us were as ignorant as they. Konosi was inclined to agree with Davati; the trolls favored the more inland track.

I was in charge. I was again the hetman. "Have you spoken to any of these northern men again?" I asked Vuk.

"That does not tell me where they live," he replied. "Only that they do live."

"And they still have heard nothing of the sorcerer," I said. Vuk only nodded.

I looked out over the rugged hills. "It matters not our exact course," I decided, "as long as we head in somewhat the correct direction. We should seek the easiest paths." If there were such.

We were closer to the mountains, standing to our left, to the west. Or they were closer to us? Closer to the coast in this region. I suspected this rough and broken land extended all the way to sea and the cliffs and fjords of which we had been told. It might not be so easy traveling along the coastline. We saw no men here, nor did we spy again the goblins. Those we all knew were about. Possibly not the same tribe as the ones we had encountered.

"The news will spread among them," felt Mug. "I would not expect trouble, but I would prepare for it." Always good advice.

"Would any trolls live in this area?" I asked him. We hiked up a valley, the shallow slopes on either side littered with broken, weathered rocks. They would be hard climbing. It was hard enough walking along the bottom.

"I think not," he replied. "Maybe further west."

"I have not felt any," added Vuk. "Never." He walked on a little before saying, "But not all troll tribes have shamans. It is an even less common gift among us than it is among men."

Mug nodded. "Some say it is not natural to trolls at all."

"Yes, from mixing with some other folk. Maybe goblins, maybe humans."

These different peoples could interbreed? It didn't seem a subject I should pry into.

Since our encounter with the goblins, Konosi had become more of a believer. Vuk had told us he spoke with the little creatures and there they were. It was becoming harder for him to remain skeptical. Whether it conflicted with his religious beliefs, I did not know. I was not even sure what those beliefs were now. But I had seen him quietly murmur a few words over a bit of acorn bread and knew he was celebrating the Christian communion. None of that on this trip — we carried only meat.

The snow was melting away. Maybe there never was that much this far north. And there was rain. Not much, but a little. I saw no reason this end of the island should have a greatly different climate than the other. The far side, across the mountains, maybe. These rains marked the beginning of summer warmth, of green spreading across the hills of the empty lands. We should not be too far now from the equinox. The day Olga suggested I wed Vasa. The reindeer would be crossing over to their summer pastures too. They had already started south when we departed.

Now we saw a little green spreading here and there in this land. Heather appeared on some of the slopes and even trees, deep in the valleys, where rushed small streams, sighing and singing across rocks and little falls. I was not completely surprised to see sheep one day, as we passed over a ridge. This looked more like home than anywhere I had seen in these empty lands. More like Russia. Not home. Not anymore.

They were small sheep, and brownish, grazing along the slopes. There must, then, be men nearby. I turned to my followers to see Vuk standing motionless, staring with unfocused eyes. I knew he was speaking from afar. To whom?

He seemed shaken when released from the spell that held him. More so than I had ever noted before. Vuk took a seat on the ground and said, "Ati called to me. I am ever ready to hear him, am listening for his voice."

He sat silently a moment, composing himself. "But it was so I might speak with Hurasu. The sorcerer had contacted Ati and the shaman wished to bring me into the link. Now, Hurasu should know me. I can listen for him too."

"But you can not speak his language," I said.

"No. Hurasu is a very great sorcerer, however, and could let me see through his eyes. He stood on a shore, looking — south, I think. There was a thing in the water that must be a boat. I do not know boats. But he is coming across the water to us. Soon."

On the mainland just north of us? Or thousands of kilometers away? How could we know? There was nothing to do but keep making our way to the sea and wait.

Below us, a man called and waved.

34. Sheep

Trolls were a great oddity here. The people knew of them but few had ever seen one. The stories many had heard made them leery of Vuk and Mug. I am not sure they completely trusted the rest of us either. Sitting down to talk and eat together put most of that to rest.

The language was largely the same. Just different enough to make for some difficulties in understanding, now and then. Only now and then. They knew we were 'Reindeer People.' Reindeer People had visited before.

He whom we had first encountered was one of the shepherds. Many were shepherds here, and both women and men attended the flocks. "My boy can guide you to the village," he had told us, turning a not particularly curious eye on the trolls. I might not have trusted my son in their company on such short acquaintance. The lad was no more than eight or nine. He was much more interested in Mug and Vuk.

"They said you were coming," the boy told us. "The shamans did." That explained some of his father's attitude. Mug entertained him with rather blood-curdling troll tales most of the way to their village. I hoped that no more than half of them were true.

Zemzem they named their village. Villages had names, unlike in the south. No shaman dwelt there. It was too small maybe. There was some sort of headman, though a council of the village elders still sat and advised and maybe overruled now and then. Gar, the headman called himself. Apparently male names were not all given a final 'i' as among the southern people. There was the breathy suggestion of a vowel.

But the people looked very much the same, whatever they were named, which is to say they looked like no particular nationality. Oh, more Caucasian than aught else, I suppose. Had all their ancestors, too, come through the way we had?

"We have sent a messenger to the closest village with a shaman," Gar informed us. We ate roast mutton with him. I can't say I liked it as well as reindeer. "He may come along here or ask you go there." Then he narrowed his eyes and lowered his voice. "The priests do not approve of all of this." Gar apparently favored the shamans. They would not challenge his authority as might priests, I decided.

"Vuk is a shaman," I told him, indicating the young troll. I was not going to suggest he try to communicate. Let Gar think of that, if he wished. The man chewed on his mutton but said nothing.

That took him up a notch in my estimation. Unless he was simply stupid. Either way, I was glad of his hospitality and that of the village, of a stomach full of mutton and a dry place to sleep. The houses here were of earth and stone, but not sunk into the ground. Even so, I made sure we remained together and one stayed on sentry through the night.

During that night, the messenger returned. His message was unnecessary, for Vuk had already spoken from afar with one shaman or another. Or maybe more than one. It did not matter. Come to Prazim, we were told. That was a larger village, further north. A center for these people, it seemed.

"Will we need a guide?" I asked Gar.

"Just follow the stream," he told me, "and ask again at the next village." Gar was short with us. Gar was not happy we were leaving and he would have no chance to play at politics with anyone. We were as willing to go as to stay, so we went. But we did thank him and the village first, and Mug had to tell another story to the assembled young and not-so-young.

I will not give you any of those here. I do not wish to disgust whoever might read this tale of mine. As it is my tale, I shall return to it.

There was a well-used path beside the stream. This stream flowed swiftly, more so than most I had seen in the south, tumbling down over many low falls. The land must fall quickly. Was it so all the way to the coast?

Always, there were sheep. When we rested, around the noontime, a pair of shepherds came and sat with us, sharing their food with us and we sharing ours with them. They had never tried reindeer before, but chewed politely on the jerky we offered. They also politely made no comment on Mug and Vuk. "We will be moving our flocks to the higher pastures soon," one told us, waving an arm toward the south. "There are good green valleys in the mountains."

113

"Some grazing is practically right up against the glaciers," added his companion.

"It is lonely up there." Both men nodded agreement to that.

We reached another village later that day and were given directions that led us along another path. We chose not to stay there but slept in the open, traveling closer to our destination while there was light. We did not need our seal-skin tents or heavy furs here.

And everywhere, we saw more sheep. Brown and gray and black, and sometimes even white, as I remembered in Russia. Too many sheep, I thought. Too many people here. This land was only a little better than further south and could not sustain a large population. It would not take much to bring famine, a bad winter, an illness among their flocks.

We journeyed on the next day and that after, seeing more villages and more sheep. Then we saw Prazim.

35. Prazim

Houses were spread below us, on the flattest land I had seen in this world. An earthen mound rose in their midst, beside a small river. Prazim was a temple center. There is no better way to describe it. We descended into the shallow valley.

That we were expected was obvious. A crowd was coming to meet us. Who was in charge here? No one seemed to be leading. Ah, a man stepped forward, a thick and swarthy fellow with a flat, almost Asiatic face, where it was not covered with black whiskers. "Welcome, travelers! I am Menig, headman of this village. The priest Pahur," he said, casually waving his left hand toward the taller man who stood beside him, "and the shaman Katira." This was an older woman at his right.

So, introductions it was. Best get the trolls first, to emphasize their importance. "This is the shaman Vuk and his protector Mug." That seemed a good title for the troll. Protector. "The priest Konosi." If we were to deal with priests then best we have one. "The hunter Misi and the hunter Davati."

Before I could put a name to myself, Konosi stepped forward, saying, "And this is Yuzi, our tsar." I had intended to say 'hetman' but it made no difference. Neither title would mean a thing to these people. Pahur gave me a quick and maybe slightly fearful look at the mention of my name. I did not know why.

But Menig seemed to accept all this with a good humored smile. Menig was a politician; that I could see at once. The crowd behind him, staring at us, looked like any other, the people the same as others in this land. Many wore leather but there was also raw uncolored woolen cloth. "Our shamans told us you were coming," he said. "They think it is very important."

"As do we," spoke Pahur. His voice was naturally high pitched but he tried to make it sound lower and more grave. It made his words a little mushy.

"Visitors from the far south are always important," proclaimed Menig. "Always welcome too."

I thought to say not that far south but held my tongue. I was not sure what to say at all. I settled for, "Thank you." Then we all trooped back down what remained of the hill and into Prazim. It would have been simpler had they waited there.

"It is auspicious that you have arrived in time for the Feast of Garun," Pahur was saying.

Konosi must have recognized I did not know what this was. "The spring equinox," he leaned in and whispered. I thought we had already passed it, to be honest.

"Indeed so," I responded, nodding gravely. "I feared we would arrive late."

"There are many pilgrims here," announced the headman. "We will see much trading." The priest's sour look said he considered this a profanation but he spoke no words.

"There will be time for all that," said Katira. "We must get our visitors settled in and rested. We have a place set aside for you," she informed me. I am not sure either Menig or Pahur was aware of this. "After a meal with our hosts of course," she added diplomatically, giving a little bow to the two men.

That soothed Menig. I'm not sure what the priest thought. It was in the headman's house we ate. It was the biggest house I had seen in this land, a long room but a narrow room with walls of undressed stone. I guessed that a narrow house would be easier to roof. Long timbers must be nearly as rare here as in the south. Rather than sod, the roofs here were covered over by a thick thatch of some coarse grass.

Not surprisingly, mutton featured in the meal. There was yogurt, too, presumably of sheep's milk, and even a soft cheese. And carrots. I did not know how much I had missed vegetables! They were a bit mushy, undoubtedly stored over winter, and maybe overcooked. Our southerners, troll and human alike, were unsure what to make of those soggy brownish-orange lumps, but Konosi and I ate more than our share, with plenty of butter. The butter certainly came from sheep milk.

I gathered we were two days away from the festival. I was not going to admit I did not know on which day it fell! The celebration would start sometime tomorrow evening. Good enough, but that was not why we

116

were here. Was there any knowledge here of Hurasu? The sooner I could see this sorcerer, speak to him, and most importantly get him to Vasa's side, the better.

It was late before we were settled in the shaman's stone hut and learned anything. Katira, flanked by a pair of younger shamans, seated herself at the central firepit and spoke. "We have tried not to tell the priests too much of Hurasu. We ourselves are fearful enough of his coming. We see a cloud at his side and what is within we can not see."

To me she then said, "Our Pahur was a bit startled by your name. It is the masculine form of a malevolent goddess, Yuza. No one here would name a child so."

"The Queen of Serpents," said the young female shaman beside her. "We do not take such things seriously."

From what Vasa had told me, maybe they should. There was no reason to bring that up right then. "Do you know when Hurasu is coming?" I asked.

Katira shook her head. "We can try speaking to him on the morrow. Now you should rest." I think we all agreed with that and were soon stretched out in the dark. The trolls snored loudly, as always. How could they not with those noses? But I lay awake a time, thinking.

Yuza. Didn't I know that name from my reading? A Turkic deity, not Indo-European. I remembered nothing else, only the name.

Ha, perhaps I should consider her my patroness. Someone who ruled over snakes could be useful, though I had seen none in this land. I slept soon and dreamed not at all.

117

36. Garun

Seven priests — all male, I noted — walked in a circle, all the way around their mound, chanting in falsetto voices while banging on frame drums or whirling bull-roarers. They wore wreathes of greenery on their heads, and skimpy loincloths about their middles, although it was rather a cold day.

The religion here seemed barely more focused than in the south. It was still more pantheistic than polytheistic. "There are hundreds of different gods known to our people," Wetos told me. "Often their duties overlap." Wetos was the other shaman who had been present the previous evening. He was also Katira's son. He and Vuk had attempted to speak with Hurasu that morning. They told us he had heard them but rejected contact. Hurasu seemed busy with something.

So the day had been spent idly. Both Menig and the priests were busy with their festival. I had told my tale in some detail to the shamans. They understood when I spoke of a gate.

And they were dismayed when I told of Vasa. "We were right about the shadow we saw," stated Katira. None of them wanted to speak further of it.

The priests were climbing their mound now, Pahur bringing up the rear. "They will remain at the top all night, seeking visions," said the shaman. "I hope they have some warm sleeping furs up there."

I doubted it. They would probably shiver through the dark and consider it a worthy devotion. "Or they might not notice the cold with the herbs they have taken," he added and, I think, snickered. Shamans had no more respect for priests here than in the south.

"What gods does your friend Konosi serve?" Wetos asked.

"The Great Father," I replied. We had decided, Konosi and I, that this was the best answer to such queries.

"Ah, the Lord of the Skies. It suits him." With the religious ceremony over and the priests all out of the way, the people turned from solemnity to celebration. The singing that arose now was far more joyous than that of the priestly procession, though nearly as tuneless. And the lyrics —

ah, I would blush if I were to repeat some of them.

"There will be several weddings tomorrow," my companion informed me. "Tonight, people will be less concerned with vows."

My people had already mixed with the crowd. Even the trolls. I did not approve but there was no sense in attempting to forbid them. I was more interested in another subject at the moment. Some of these folk were avidly drinking — something. Did they have alcohol here?

"Fermented milk," Wetos told me. It didn't sound so good but I shouldn't decide without trying it, should I? It tasted better and better as the evening went on. I got to my bed sometime before dawn, only to be shaken awake at what seemed almost immediately to me.

"The priests will come down and give their prophecies in a few minutes." It was the other shaman, the girl. What was her name? She was young, and Katira's apprentice. We went out into the half-light of early morning to see the priests filing down the side of their mound. Each in turn told of what he had seen in the night.

The pronouncements were about as to expected. Predictions of the blessing of the gods and of many lambs being born and happiness running rampant. What the people wanted and what the priests might actually believe they had seen. Drugs and expectations would work together to ensure that.

Until Pahur, the last, spoke. "A god came to me in the night," he called out. He did not attempt to lower his pitch this morning, his voice ringing high and clear. "He warned of an evil sorcerer on his way here, one named Hurasu!" There were murmurs. Rumors of the name had already been floating about and even older stories that had named such a man.

Pahur's pitch went even higher. "His servants have already come to greet him and aid him in his evil. They work with the Queen of Serpents!" He pointed toward me, of course. At which moment, a broad hand grabbed my arm. "We'd best get you out of here, boy," said Menig. "Yon priest has taken too much of the wrong herbs."

The crowd was milling about, uncertain. Most were a bit bleary-eyed and not inclined to action right then. Maybe after a nap. Menig and the girl hurried me back to Katira's house. I was pleased to see the rest of my group still snoring there. We filled in Wetos and his mother, as quickly and succinctly as we could.

"Why would he decide to make such a claim?" I asked. I assumed he lied but could not understand the reason.

Katira spoke slowly and carefully. "Evil dreams might have been sent to him by a powerful sorcerer. He whom we sensed in the cloud by Hurasu maybe — he who harmed your woman, Yuzi."

Menig spat. He was polite enough to do it into the fire pit rather than on the floor. "Bad business," he mumbled. He might have meant more than one thing by that. "We'd best get the lot of you out of town right now. Up to the coast?" This he directed at Katira.

The shaman nodded. "That is where they would have met Hurasu anyway. Someone should go with them." She looked at her son a moment, and then at her apprentice.

"Ashaga," she decided. "You will guide them."

37. Ashaga

We were gone within the hour. If Pahur ever managed to organize anyone to pursue us, we did not see them. I do not think his own mind was
very well organized that morning. We hurried north for a couple hours
before Ashaga held up a hand. "It is time Vuk and I tried to speak with
Hurasu again." She paused, frowned just enough to make two little lines
above her strong nose. "And maybe others."

Tell her mistress that all was well. Of course she should do that. The
girl was young, maybe as young as Vasa, but dark and robust rather than
thin and pale. She looked a little like the headman of Prazim, I decided.
Maybe a relative. She and Vuk sat facing each other for a little while, all
their attention turned elsewhere. "He still refuses us," Vuk said at last.

"So we must guess where he will come," said Ashaga, rising. "Not to
the coast due north of here. That is closest for us but there is no good
landing there." She knew of harbors? That was valuable. Perhaps that
was why Katira sent her with us.

"And all is well otherwise?" I asked. She only nodded.

"We should move more northwest now," the girl said. "Toward the
northern points and the bays that lie there." Yes, she definitely knew of
harbors. "It will take many days," she added, almost apologetically.

"Then we shall have the pleasure of your company for a longer time,"
said Konosi. I did not know he had it in him. The land did not change
much at first. There were still plenty of sheep too; we seemed to spy a
new flock every time were crossed over one of the low rounded ridges
here. But it did over the days grow more rugged and rocky and the
mountains pressed closer to our left.

We found hospitality wherever we went. If the priests of Prazim disliked us, it seemed to have gone no farther than their town. Sometimes
there would be a local shaman who knew of us. Some of these looked
upon our group with some nervousness, and not just because of the
trolls. Those certainly aroused attention everywhere. "They are all — no,
we are all uncertain about Hurasu's coming," said Ashaga. "And what
may come with him."

The young shaman was willing to talk with any of us as we walked along. All of us were quite as willing to talk back — Davati and Misi the most, maybe. Ashaga was not unattractive and she was, after all, the only girl there. This afternoon, she walked beside me. "Tell me of Vasa," she said. I did not know what to say but she pried a story from me, asking the right questions when I faltered or fell silent. That is part of a shaman's training too, I understand.

"She is very powerful," the girl said at last. "So very much more powerful than I." She did not put enough inflection on any of this for me to tell how she felt about it.

"Does that matter?" I asked.

She laughed. Her laugh was hearty, deep. "Not at all, Tsar Yuzi. I am happy with my own gift." Her eyes went to Konosi. "Is the priest happy? He seems so solemn at times."

"He finds happiness in solemnity," I said, with a wink. "I think he finds some happiness walking with you, as well." I had noticed.

"But he is looking for something and has not yet found it."

"I think he has lost his god," I said, serious now. "The god he knew in our world."

"Ah. Then he has lost himself as well." She spoke no more on that, but did walk at Konosi's side later.

It was the next day, near noon, when the priest leaned in and asked, "Do you smell the sea?"

I had not noticed, but yes. The sea's presence was in the air, carried on a light breeze out of the northeast. "How near, I wonder?"

"Ashaga probably knows. She's from around here." The girl had not told me this.

We were on a true road now, winding among steep valley walls. They reminded me of old Chinese paintings. This was the first area I had seen which might actually be called forested, with the valley depths filled with tall conifers. "I believe we have moved into a marine forest sort of climate here," was Konosi's opinion.

"I do not know what that means," Ashaga commented, "but it is a forest and the sea is not far away. We come near to our land's northern tip, where three great points spread like a crane's toes. We will turn aside before we reach them."

It was the next morning, a drizzly gray morning where the steep hills rose up of a sudden from the mist, that we at last stood above the sea. Far below us it lay, stretching sullen and dark, beyond two deep bays. A point jutted between them. On that finger of land we could see buildings. "That's where I grew up," said Ashaga. "That is Akmem."

38. Akmem

"So Uncle Menig got them out of there as quickly as he could," Ashaga concluded.

"Fools, like all priests," spat her father. Such vehemence contrasted with his mild appearance.

Ashaga gave Konosi a sidelong glance and snickered. "Father is a shaman. You must expect such from him."

"Perhaps priests from other worlds are different," the man allowed. He peered at Konosi. "You don't take those herbs, do you?"

"Only wine, if I could find any," responded the tall priest. He had to invent a word for wine, combining those for 'fruit' and the fermented milk beverage we had imbibed at Prazim.

Ashaga's mother laughed. I could readily see that she was Menig's sister. "We have *vino* here. Grape vines grow well on this coast." Masaga was her name.

I could believe in those vines. It did seem just the sort of climate for them, here at the northern tip of the island. The word vino might well have come straight from our own Russian tongue. I believed even more when she fetched us some in a leather bag.

Akmem was not a particularly large village, certainly not near the size of Prazim. It was, however, a center for several small towns around these two bays, occupied by both herdsmen and those who fished. It was central, standing on these heights and looking toward both harbors. It was also the first village I had seen that was fortified, with stone walls all around.

The houses were of stone too. Some were all of stone, beehive huts. The shaman Ilar, Ashaga's father, had a large house with more normal roofing, and an extended family to live in it. Ashaga had many brothers and sisters, and nieces and nephews too. None had shown a shamanic gift save her.

"So," said Ilar, after we had passed the bag of wine around, "should we try to talk to this wizard?"

"All three of us?" asked Vuk. He had sipped the wine, made a rather hideous troll face, and handed it on.

"Why not?" said the shaman. "You know where to look for him, right?" Both Vuk and Ashaga nodded.

But I asked that they first try to contact Ati or even Vuk's mentor Zup and see how things went in the south. For some reason, Ati could not be reached. He could simply be asleep or not listening. Knowing that did not keep me from worrying. Zup knew nothing, according to Vuk. The other two could not understand the old troll shaman, of course.

It was decided to eat again before trying to reach Hurasu. We were served mutton, not surprisingly, but also a variety of seafood, all cooked up together in a stew — fish and squid and clams, for certain, and perhaps some other things. Carrots, too. More wine. The trolls did not accept a second taste but Konosi and our hunters enjoyed it.

Near dark it was when our shamans settled down to their task, the three sitting facing each other. I knew that didn't make any difference. Vasa had told me it would all work just as well back-to-back or in different rooms or on opposite sides of the world. Where they were going mattered, not where they were.

I assumed the trio had met up in some other world, one of those safe places of which I had been told. Then they would seek Hurasu, and he might come to them or they might go to him. Or something. I can only try to make sense of things I have not experienced myself. Occasionally, some slight change of expression or a subtle movement of head or hands indicated the activity within. Mostly they sat immobile, eyes half-closed and unfocused.

Ilar was the first to come out of it. Practice and experience, maybe. He sat quietly, waiting for the other two to return. "You got that?" he asked his daughter. She nodded. Vuk seemed bewildered.

"He could not tell us anything, so Hurasu attempted to show us things through his own eyes," Ashaga told us.

"A dangerous thing," mumbled Vuk.

"It is," Ilar agreed. "I would not attempt it myself. I recognized what he showed us."

"As did I," said Ashaga. "He is on a boat, preparing to land on the western coast. Almost due west of here, I think."

Her father nodded an agreement. "We tried to tell him we would come to him," he said. "We do not know if he understood."

"Then we must follow the coast around to him?" I asked. "Or cross the mountains?"

One of Ilar's sons spoke up. "No need. There are many boats here. I can take you."

Konosi laughed. "So we might as well have come in a boat from the start!"

"Don't be foolish," admonished Ashaga. "Then how would you ever have met me?"

39. The Crane's Foot

Toes on a crane's foot, Ashaga had said, so were the three peninsulas at this island's northern end. We would sail around two of these; Hurasu's landing would be north of the third. Or so she and her father were fairly sure. The first toe made up the far side of the bay that lay just north of Akmem.

It was no surprise to see a skin boat not unlike the ones we had used in the south. Better and more solidly framed with wood however, which was not so scarce up here. It belonged to the husband of Masaga's sister, as far as I could make out, a big man named Savur. He asked no price for its use. "If Ilar says it is needed, it is needed," he said. Savur did insist on coming along to pilot it.

Yes, it belonged to the man. Things were not owned in common up here. Tashi, Ashaga's brother, came along too as crew. The hunters stayed behind. There was no room — six was enough and we might need to bring Hurasu back. Six. That is right. Ashaga was not to go with us. We had Vuk if a shaman were needed; there was no point in risking the girl. And, again, there was the matter of space.

I was happy to see a sail. It was primitive and rectangular, wider than it was tall, but it meant less paddling. "The winds should be favorable going," was Savur's opinion. It needn't be said then that they would be less so coming back. Out of the deep long bay we paddled, the high cliffs to our left blocking much in the way of a wind. Four of us paddled; our two trolls were still attempting to deal with being on the water for the first time in their lives.

As short as they were, they would have had difficulty reaching the water anyway. We passed the headland and a breeze came up, from the northeast. "We can use that," felt Savur, hoisting his woolen sail and quartering across the wind. With no keel to steady the boat beneath that sail, it wallowed greatly. The seas were not small and spray blew from the wave tops. Konosi loved it, I think. Me, not so much.

The trolls just got sick and looked grayer than ever.

But it was fast going. The coast curved back in on the other side of the 'toe' but Savur held us away from it, steering far out to sea, much further out than Mazi and his men of the sea had ever been willing. There was no need to paddle, other than for steering, and Tashi and Savur could handle that. Konosi and I did spend a lot of time bailing sea water from the bottom of the craft. We rounded the second toe as the sea fell into darkness.

I had assumed we would pull ashore for the night. I should not have. "We shall be sheltered behind the point," explained Tashi. He looked up. "It's clear enough we could probably steer by the stars." He pointed to three stars, lined up low in the sky. "Beyana's Arrow. It ever points south." I did not know who or what Beyana was. A woman's name in form. We did paddle a little through the night to hold our course, not vigorously, and Savur lowered his sail.

I slept eventually. I had not intended to; I simply started awake and realized I had. There was a suggestion of dawn above the dark mountain peaks to our left. The sea was relatively calm here. "Your man's landing place should not be too far ahead," announced Savur. "We'll move in close and keep a watch for him." He paused and scanned the east. "And anyone else. There can be danger in all waters and more over here."

"Hurasu should already have landed, right?" This I directed to Vuk.

"I think so," came his slow response, his voice low and a little weak. "He seemed as close to the shore as we are now." And that was two days ago. "I shall seek him." He sat down in the bottom of the boat to do just that.

This sorcerer expected us. That's what our shamans had thought, anyway. He would not go off somewhere else when we were coming. Vuk made keening noises, which may have had more to do with seasickness than his trance, and opened his eyes. "Hurasu is on the beach. A beach. There was no way to tell me just where." A shrug. "He was completely open to me today. I do not know why that has changed."

"So we find this fellow," said Savur. "Hmm, there might be enough breeze coming down the hills for the sail." He spent some time getting it up. The rest of us paddled. It was Mug who spied the other boats, pointing them out, closer to the beaches than we. Not Hurasu, surely?

Three hide boats, not unlike our own, but without sails. Many men wielded paddles, directing them straight at us. "They mean us no good," muttered Konosi.

"Savages. Cannibals." Savur grabbed a paddle. "There would be no fighting them." We saw the wisdom in running. Even the trolls paddled as best they could. Not that we could escape. Not on the water. There was not enough wind for the sail to give us an advantage, and not enough arms to propel us. I could see forest on the shore, flat land and beaches. If we could get onto land maybe we could hide. A slight chance but better than we faced at sea.

"A boat," cried out Tashi, pointing to the beach. Some sort of long craft was pulled up onto the sands. Friends? Enemies? It didn't matter. We knew they could be no worse than those who pursued us. Those I could not make out except as dark distant figures. I hoped they remained such.

Savur drove his boat toward the beach. Sand, not rock — that was certainly good fortune! We leaped out, spears in hands, as soon as the bottom scraped. Could we make it to the cover of the trees? I didn't take time to look at the other craft on the beach except to quickly realize it was a dugout canoe. We were not halfway to the forest when our pursuers were bounding onto the beach in our wake. I made my decision. "Go on," I yelled to my companions, as I turned, unslung the rifle on my back, and knelt, ready to fire.

The sound of running feet behind. Approaching? The idiots! They had no chance. Let me slow them down, and run for cover! I spied someone from the corner of my eye. A lithe, black-haired man stood there. In his hand was a sword, a long gleaming metal sword. Though I had not seen him before, even in visions, I knew this was Hurasu.

Now the rest of my party came up to stand beside me, and three other men I knew not. Two of those carried bows. Then I had to act, for the attackers were nearly on us. They had not slowed at all, running straight forward, screaming some sort of war cries. I shot the foremost man — he looked more or less like a man — and none slowed down. My second shot hit someone, I think, and then I had to toss the rifle aside and prepare to fight with spear.

I was only slightly aware that arrows had also been speeding toward that mob. Some had dropped but more ran on. Hurasu leaped forward and waded into them, the sword swinging accurately and deadly. I followed as best I could, spear ready.

No need. Almost as one, our opponents howled and turned tail. A few arrows were sent in their wake. It could only have been this man with his shining sword who had so disheartened them. If one had never seen such a weapon it might seem as magic. It might be seen as wielded by a god. I looked at the bodies they had left behind. They did not quite seem men. "Anyone hurt?" I called out.

Apparently not. We had barely begun to engage them when this whirlwind with his silver blade had sent them running. I looked him over. Not a big man, no taller than I. His black hair and beard were closely cropped and a hawk-like nose jutted beneath the raven brows. The skin was as Vasa had described, as the color of old parchment.

He reached down and picked up my discarded Mosin Nagant. Did he know what it was? Apparently, for he shouldered the rifle and sighted down the barrel before smiling and returning it to me.

Vuk and Mug were looking over the bodies and casually dispatching any that still clung to life. "Troll-men," growled Mug. "Raiding from the far south."

Troll-men. Yes, they did look like — like hybrids. Yet, in some way, more bestial than either man or troll. "Full of herbs to madden them," whispered Vuk. Mug only nodded grimly. Hurasu was following the two with his eyes, the ghost of a grim smile on his lips. He spoke to them in a language no one understood.

So I spoke to him in my own. "Greetings to you, Hurasu," I said. It seemed as good a way to begin as any.

40. Learning

Hurasu's two bowmen were bronzed wiry warriors with Asiatic features. They spoke no language we understood but he could converse with them. To his third retainer he spoke what seemed a completely different tongue. This man was quite dark but had a mop of disconcertingly blond curling hair.

"African?" I murmured, mostly to myself. That didn't seem right.

"Australoid, I think," said Konosi. Yes, he was right. I could see that. Some of them did have blond hair, didn't they?

We went back to our boat to pull it to a safer spot — the tides here rose and fell prodigiously — and get our belongings. Then we followed Hurasu to his camp. I did eye his big dugout. It was all of one great log, and with curiously carved figures along its prow.

The camp was simple. I think Hurasu had little need of luxuries. We chewed on some dried fish while he regarded us. Then he began addressing us, in one unknown language after another. He was quite patient. When one received no response, he went on to the next. Suddenly, a surprised Konosi answered the latest attempt with a few broken words. It sounded slightly familiar to me.

"Greek," explained the priest. "A very ancient sort of Greek." The two exchanged a few more words. "He is going to try some others. If we don't know any, my bad Greek will have to do."

As it was, I knew the next attempt. I think maybe Hurasu suspected one of us would. It was English. My English is not good but it is better than Konosi's Greek. No, that is unfair. Better than Konosi's ancient Greek.

"I learned this language from another who came through a gate, two decades ago," Hurasu said. "That gate is on the other side of the world. He came from a land called America. Is that your home?"

I shook my head. "No, I lived near the gate we passed through. Our land is the Sov — ah, Russia. I learned English but it is not my native tongue."

"Then I shall speak English with you until I can learn the language here. You will teach me." He smiled. "And translate."

That was alright with me. I would do whatever it took to get him to Vasa. "Then we can begin our journey," I said.

"Yes. I need to learn your language quickly so I can speak to the — what do you call them here, wizards?"

"Shamans," I told him.

"Ah, yes, that makes sense. I have known shamans." Hurasu chuckled softly. "I speak regularly with one who lives on the far side of this world."

"As do you?" I asked.

He nodded. "I have been careful of making contact with your shamans for I would take no chance of repeating what happened with Vasa."

"I do not understand that," I admitted.

"Neither do I. It surely has something to do with the gate." He paused, pensive. "It was because of the gate that I was already on my way here but what I learned from Vasa hurried me."

He turned to the two lean warriors who had accompanied him, speaking a few words. They replied but a few words in a guttural tongue, bowed, and left. "I have released them," he told me. "Our covenant was for them to bring me here. They have done so, and will now take their canoe and return to their home in the north. I will travel with you." He nodded toward his remaining retainer. "I and Thun."

I translated this for the others, as I had been doing off and on already. When it seemed important; after all, I remained the one in charge. Ha, the truth is that as soon as Hurasu appeared he was in charge. We all knew that. By that evening, he had made a start on our language. Hurasu was a quick learner.

The lessons continued the next day, as we prepared to leave, as we paddled north. Constant they were, Hurasu insisting on learning every minute. Although the winds were not too bad, our voyage home was days longer than our journey to find the wizard. There was far too much paddling, and too much sleeping in a cramped, rocking boat. By the time we reached Akmem, Hurasu was nearly as good in his new language as in English.

Thun had picked up a smattering too. "Thun is a sorcerer," Mug had whispered to me one evening. "Vuk senses it." Two of them then. Maybe

Thun was some sort of apprentice. A nice breeze came to fill our sail as we entered the bay and approached the place from which we had started.

Hurasu sat quietly for but a moment. I hardly noted it. "I have informed the shaman here that we have arrived," he announced. "I felt I knew the language well enough now to do this." His smile was just slightly smug.

We never spoke English again.

41. Nagi

"My ancestors came from a land your ancestors knew as Atlantis. I heard legends of it in your world but doubt it ever existed there." Konosi and I could follow this. To the others here, the name Atlantis meant nothing.

"It was a world of great sorcerers," continued Hurasu, "of towers that brushed the sky and golden cities spread below them. I yet recall the dawns when twin suns rose together, their lights mingling subtly on the languid seas. I coveted power then, to be one of those who ruled, and reaching for the prize, failed.

"So it was I fled that world, the world of my birth, and found my way to that of yours. I knew of a gate; it was the easiest, the quickest, escape, and I needed that! Not knowing whether I might come through to land or water, I opened my way standing in a gilded gondola I had stolen. I felt quite foolish to find myself standing in it in the middle of dry hills.

"In Anatolia that was, and I wandered your world for three centuries, seeking a way to another, for my power was weak there. It is not a world of magic, as you know. At last, in the land of the Scythians, I found my gate opened by the power of the storm and came through — to here."

"This was long ago," Konosi murmured.

"Two thousands of years," he replied. "Yes, my people are long-lived. Some say there is the blood of the fay in us."

"And you came to this island, as did we," I said.

"There were fewer humans here then. Those who had passed through that gate, and those descended from them, made their way elsewhere when able. I did the same. After a time." He seemed far away for a moment. "A small tribe I encountered here named the land Nagi, meaning 'sorrow' in their language. I lived with them a while, married a woman who grew old and died. Then I moved on."

None of us had anything to say to that. Hurasu took another slice of mutton from the wooden platter. "There were no sheep here when last I visited. Reindeer, yes. They were always here. They may have come across a land bridge in a far distant past. But sheep have been brought later by men."

"You came back?" asked Ashaga.

"I returned once, a few hundred years ago, and traveled around Nagi to get a sense of its size and shape. It is a large island. Some might even call it a continent. As a great crescent it lies in the seas, the far side sloping down to a wide bay. No, call it a gulf; it is large enough."

This caught Konosi's imagination. "I would like sometime to sail all the way around." He turned to me. "Will we sail home or walk?"

I had assumed we would go back the way we came. A water route had not even occurred to me. "We would have to borrow Savur's boat again," I said. I am sure I did not sound very enthusiastic. "How many will we be?" I started to count in my head.

"You can skip Davati," said Ashaga. "He met a girl he likes and plans to stay." She grinned. "But I can take his place in the crew."

"Should you not return to your apprenticeship?" asked her father.

"When I can learn from the greatest sorcerer in the world?" It was a good counter.

"We shall build a new boat," declared Tashi. "Bigger!"

"No time," I answered. I wanted to be gone at once. If a boat were not available, we would start walking. Hurasu looked capable of long hikes, no matter how old he was.

"We shall take two boats," the sorcerer stated. And with that it was settled.

I liked the idea of two. It made me fell safer. They were procured the next day. Haggling is a roundabout affair in a barter economy! I am not sure even now exactly who paid for them — or how. Sheep were involved somehow. They were good enough boats, the same sort as Savur's but a little smaller. I made sure they had sails. No paddling all the way south. We would launch from the other bay, the one that lay south of Akmem. The boats were quite light and easy to portage from one to the other.

I and Konosi, Mug and Vuk and Misi. That was five from our original expedition. So I thought. The trolls came to me and said they would rather walk home. "What of the goblins," I asked, "and all the land of men here in the north?"

"What of all that water?" replied Mug. "We will stay to the mountains.

We know other troll tribes there." So five became three. Then Hurasu and his apprentice, and Ashaga. Six. Six until Tashi insisted on coming along. I think his parents wanted him to keep an eye on his sister. We would leave on the morrow, as early as practical.

It was growing late and I stood looking out at the bay. Summer was coming; the sun lingered later each evening. I thought maybe I would see these people and this town again someday. The lands that lay north of Nagi called to me. Now I'd best return to the house of Ilar and share one more meal with his family. I descended from the low stone wall surrounding the village, into deep shadow. That shadow suddenly seemed to writhe, like snakes of dark smoke, twining and twisting, and fading — and allowing a strange woman to step out of their midst before they dissipated into nothing.

She was dressed as a woman of the steppes, a Tatar, and her face was as the sun, with strong high cheekbones. Tall, she was, and more beautiful than any woman I had ever seen. Or so I thought at the time. Later I could not quite recall why. "So this is the one the priests have been whispering about," she said, looking me up and down. "The one who wears my name."

Her name? Who was she? Some sort of shaman?

"Ah, he is confused," she laughed. "The man knows nothing of goddesses."

Goddesses — her name — I felt my heart attempting to hide in my stomach. "Yuza," I said.

"He understands now! Handsome *and* smart."

"The name is but an accident," I said.

"So I know, Yuzi. Your name came from another world and has naught to do with me." I was glad she was talking to me instead of about me now. "The priests are quite stupid. They are not my priests, anyway." She made an exaggeratedly sad face. "No one wants to be my priest."

At that moment, I was ready to volunteer for the job. As I said before, I do not remember why. "You are called the Queen of Serpents." It was a notably stupid thing to say.

Her laugh was as golden as she. "I do not really have much to do with snakes," she said, smirking oh so slightly. "Think of them as symbolic."

136

Of what? Oh! Of course. Yuza was a goddess of sex. I had been told she seduced men at an alarming rate. That may have been wishful thinking by men who had seen her.

She must have known what I was thinking. "That is not why I am here, Man Who Stole My Name. Not that I would mind much." Yuza sort of giggled at that, but sobered immediately. "There is sorcery gathering and I like it not. It is upsetting things."

"Hurasu?" I asked.

"He would seek to set things right, I think." Yuza apparently knew the man was there. "There is another we can not see, and some disturbance of the ways between worlds." She looked sharply at me. "This has touched you, has it not?"

"The one I love has been harmed by this, um, one you can not see."

The goddess seemed to be looking somewhere else for a moment, somewhere beyond the sight of men. "Vasa. Hmm. Not so much love as duty, I think. I might try to steal love but I would not keep a warrior from his duty."

"This warrior will welcome any help he can get." Even from a snake goddess or whatever she was.

"Who could say? Maybe the gods will help. I was only sent to learn." She laughed. "My family knows I am good at getting things from men."

Smoke writhed again, snakes of smoke, and Yuza disappeared among them. I went into the house of Ilar. Hurasu gave me a quite knowing look.

42. The Empty Coast

Perhaps Yuza was right. I was seeing Vasa as much as a duty as someone I loved. But a man needs a purpose. I have said this before.

We launched our boats into the morning mists. Hurasu said nothing to me of visitors, much less goddesses. There may have been no reason to. He and I and Thun would travel in the boat piloted by Tashi; Konosi would take charge of the other boat, with Ashaga and Misi. Our intent was to stay as close together as possible.

I was already thinking of this island as Nagi, as Hurasu had called it. No one living here had seemed to have a name for the whole of it. I like having names for things. We would sail mostly east for some time, along the northern coasts of Nagi, before rounding a great cape and turning south, seeking the bay near our village, the bay where Mazi and the other men of the sea had their home.

"We should be about even with the coast north of Prazim," announced Tashi near dusk. "It might be well to put into the harbor there." The young man was not enthusiastic about spending the night at sea. We had dealt with fickle winds all the day and who knew where they might blow through the darkness?

And we wanted to keep the boats together. I was not sure we were as far along in our journey as he had estimated, nor did I want to search for a landing place in the growing dark. What if those there were hostile to us? They could know of the priests' animosity. "No," I decided. I must be the one who decided and that should be understood right now — not even Hurasu could overrule me here. "Lash the boats together and we shall try to maintain our course overnight."

That meant some must stay awake and use the paddles to keep us moving eastward, as well as away from the now-invisible shore. No sails, of course. Konosi gave a look of approval. The others simply obeyed.

"This coast is empty," remarked Hurasu as we resumed our journey the next morning. The winds were better today, though we had to angle into the predominantly northeasterly flow. The sails were notably inefficient for this. "Nagi has not changed so much in most places. It remains inhospitable."

"We rarely sail this direction," said Tashi, "except to fish. More often, it is north to the other islands."

"To the mainland?" asked the sorcerer.

Our pilot shook his head. "Never have I voyaged that far. Some do."

"Much land is empty there too." His eyes went briefly to me. "It beckons those for whom Nagi has grown too small. Hmm?" Hurasu's attention was directed toward the other boat, close alongside. Ashaga was sitting erect, eyes closed.

Then she returned to us. "Our friend Vuk wished me to tell you his journey goes well. Already he and Mug are high in the mountains," she called out. I shouted a thanks in return.

"A decent talent," Hurasu murmured, more to himself than anyone else. Then he smiled and commented, "Quite probably one of my descendants. I have been in this world so long almost everyone is."

"The Father of Sorcerers," said Thun. He rarely said anything, in part because he was not as advanced in our language.

"That is possibly true, as well," admitted Hurasu. "It may be my heritage that gives this gift."

"But not to Vasa," I said.

Another of Hurasu's enigmatic yet somehow superior smiles. "It is not to be assumed I remained celibate for my three hundred years in your world, Yuzi. But there could be other sources." The smile disappeared. "The fact that Vasa sensed things even in that other world shows how powerful she is."

Ati had said something similar to me, hadn't he? Someone had.

"I could teach her much," Hurasu continued. "She should not remain in this land." I saw Thun give his master a knowing look. 'Thun,' I had learned, meant 'Number One' in their language — a title, not a name. He was Hurasu's chief lieutenant or something of that sort.

On we sailed, along that rock-bound empty coast, day following day. I felt some sympathy for Ashaga as the only woman here. Women, in my experience, liked some privacy. Even in this land. Oh, I guess we men did too. She heard requests from time to time to look the other direction.

A wide bay opened to our right; it would not have made a good harbor, being too open, but it could have served if necessary. "Had we walked straight north we might reached the sea about here," felt Misi. The young hunter seemed to have a bit of an internal compass. Konosi nodded an agreement with this. Then the coast turned back to the north some, as we approached the cape.

Or, more accurately, as we coasted along its northern side. The seas seemed to grow increasingly turbulent, with the swells coming from more than one direction and sometimes combining to create great feathering peaks before again going their ways. "We are more exposed to the ocean here," Hurasu informed us. He knew far more of this world than any of us; indeed, we knew almost nothing beside a man who had explored it for two thousand years! "There is a great expanse of empty water that direction." He pointed to the northeast.

"Do you live on the far side?" I asked.

"I suppose I do. It is easier for me to travel here from the other direction," Hurasu answered. "The home I chose for myself, long ago, lies closer to that other gate I mentioned. Ocean is to be found at both ends of it, so only those who sail have passed through."

That, I decided, was a story to ask for some other time. A wind was coming up, a strong headwind. The sails became more hindrance than aid in our progress, and were lowered. We paddled, progressing slowly against the power of the gale. "A storm of the south," felt Tashi. "The wind will come around soon and blow down from the mountains and across the sea." He considered for a moment before saying to me, "This time we should seek harbor." I knew it to be good advice.

But how much further could we go before taking it? Could we first round the cape, perhaps use that wind to carry us down the other side? When the coast began to sweep due north, standing in unbroken cliffs, I decided not to attempt it. One of the fjords should give us shelter. Let us hope an itzo did not lurk in its depths, eh?

Our refuge was little more than a narrow crack in the cliffs. That was to the good. We were well protected. It ran back into the face, the water lying deep and black below us. Too narrow for the itzo, maybe. Not a good place for its ambush hunting. So I told myself! Between the high walls and sky of storm, no light reached us, huddled in our flimsy boats, tied together close to the sheer cliffs.

"One of we who have powers could probably pull in some illumination from another world," whispered Hurasu. I heard him laugh. "I could anyway, and Thun. Our shaman has not been trained in such things."

"Can this be done?" Ashaga's voice wafted from the other boat.

"It is not easy and rarely worth the effort. For a sorcerer, that is. Gods do such things as second nature." Another laugh, short. "Or maybe it is their first nature. I have always made it a policy to avoid gods."

"Easier to bring a flame from somewhere and light our own lamp from it." That was Thun's voice. I felt around. We did have a stone lamp somewhere among our baggage, and ample fat to burn in it. I would not have attempted to light it in the wind and rain, even protected some as we were. Perhaps Thun could. I found it, wrapped in a bit of seal skin, and passed it to him.

"It will need to be a strong spark on this night," spoke Hurasu. "Nor is there any guarantee it will stay lit."

It might. It was a lamp made for the sea, with protection for its flame, a sort of flue carved into the soft volcanic stone. An almost blinding white light flashed; as our eyes adjusted, a warmer glow from the lamp appeared.

"Ah, lightning!" Hurasu's voice held admiration. "That was well done, Thun. And most foolhardy."

I could see Thun's dark face, his curling beard, the heavy brows, as he held the lamp before him with both hands, trying to turn it where least affected by the wind. He looked pleased with what he had done. Then, a look of surprise on that face, followed by one of terror. The lamp fell, the light disappeared.

At once, another light, almost like sunlight, poured forth like a beam from — from where? Hurasu's outstretched palm? So it seemed. With his other hand, he yanked the long silver sword from its sheath. Thun struggled in the prow, something wrapped about his body. A great tentacle it was, fully a foot through, a sickly pinkish-gray. A vast saucer-shaped alien eye glittered momentarily in the dark water. Hurasu lunged forward.

Too late. His man was dragged from the boat, instantly disappearing into the hidden depths. The great squid, the giant of deep places. Had I not been warned of it, long before? "The kraken." Hurasu let his light, the light pulled from some other world, go out. "The lamp must have attracted it."

"Will it return?" I was not sure who spoke. Maybe Misi.

"I think not, if we remain in the dark and move little," said the sorcerer. Then, a great sigh. "I think, too, I shall need a new Thun."

43. Homecoming

Hurasu had many Thuns in the course of his tremendously long life. This he told me later. Men and women, all drawn from the people of the great valley where he ruled, a land where sorcery was more common than anywhere else in the world. They were not administrators or lieutenants so much as his chief wizards, those who attended to all the details of such things. Hurasu had no time for that.

He was saddened but did not let grief linger. I could not imagine how many lives he had seen come and go in the course of his own. Could such a man truly have friends? He would regret our passing as we might regret that of a beloved dog.

Why were there no dogs on Nagi? I wondered that briefly. We had found our way back to the sea the next day, the storm passed but a powerful wind at our backs. That would help us round the cape but going might be hard on the far side. "We must stay close to the shore and paddle in the protection of the cliffs," advised Konosi. It was probably good advice but we would not know until we reached the east side.

But the wind grew less over time. We had it when we needed it and not so much after that. One might call it good fortune but, of course, that is how storm winds are. They do not last. In three days, the more normal northeasterly flow had returned and helped us the rest of the way. The coast was much as on the other side of the cape — as we had been told before by those who lived by the sea. Rocky, cleft by deep narrow bays, high cliffs standing league after league. It was not so long until we rounded a point and spied the familiar bay, the one Konosi and I had stood beside on the solstice night.

In a day we could be with Vasa. We had made haste, as we could. There was no need to rush now, I told myself. All will be well with Hurasu here at last.

"All the way from the crane's foot?" asked Mazi. "That is a great voyage!" He had stood on the beach, watching, as we sailed the last kilometer across the bay. Mazi knew the crane's foot only through second hand accounts, but he did know it was a journey that far exceeded any the men here would attempt. We certainly went up in his estimation.

He was also greatly interested in the sails, as he nor any of the others had ever used them. Later, Hurasu confided, "I learned something of sails and sailing from the man of whom I told you."

"The one from America."

"Yes. I could show these people a little of that, after we attend to our business here." His face hardened, almost imperceptibly. "That must come first." On that I was in complete agreement — if our business was the same.

Ashaga immediately became an item of business for the many bachelors here. She handled it well. Better than Konosi. He scowled much at the young men who followed her about. Was he thinking of marrying this girl? I admit to knowing little of priests and the Orthodox Church. I was pretty sure the priests did marry. Some of them. I was not so sure if Konosi even considered himself bound by his religion's rules anymore.

But I am turning onto a side path there. Of more immediate importance to me was that Ashaga took the time to speak with Vuk, and assured me the trolls were still traveling. Moreover, they were taking their time, visiting other tribes, and Vuk himself might have found a willing troll-girl to go home with him. They certainly had a better time of their journey than we.

Six we were, but others joined us on the trek to the village. Some dozen men waited in the first light of morning, some with business, some simply bored with life by the sea and more than willing to walk all day with a nice-looking young woman. Mazi came too. He wanted to hear more of our voyage though we had talked of it all the evening before.

Maybe it should have felt like a homecoming. I found I felt no attachment to this place, nor much more to these people. It all seemed as impersonal as the army had been, only duty. Oh, I know some soldiers saw it as more. To them, serving Mother Russia was as being part of a family. I never desired that, never felt a need to belong. As I had never desired to stand out or be noticed. It was far too late for that here!

Bah. Maybe I would see it differently tomorrow. I had been gone too long, had too many concerns pulling my thoughts elsewhere. Maybe I was just a little pleased to see the earthen houses at last. But it was one house and the girl within it that was foremost in my mind. I led Hurasu directly to old Ati's abode. It seems all the others followed us, as well as a crowd that formed.

Ati himself sat before his doorway. He narrowed his eyes and peered at Hurasu. "Hmmph, here at last," was his only comment.

"How is Vasa?" was mine.

"See for yourself. Vasa!" he called over his shoulder. "Your man has returned." Ati chuckled. "She has recovered all on her own."

Yes, she looked — well, better, I thought, as she came out to us. Recovered? I was not so sure. "Josef!" She came into my arms.

Frail, she felt, but Vasa had always been slight. "It is good to be back," I told her.

"Stay this time," she whispered into my chest.

44. One Within

"The other one is still with her," Hurasu told me. I had been about to go to sleep but this changed my plan. "Or more precisely," he continued, "a part of Vasa is in another place with him."

He had sat some time with the girl in the evening, speaking to her with no words. As I understood it, they, too, were in some other place. "I had hoped to go further into her mind but I saw the danger of it. I would be detected by this other and he would know that I was aware of him. So I retreated, acting as though nothing was amiss."

"I thought you only, um, spoke in those places you go," I said. Not that I truly knew anything of it.

"It is possible," he said, seeming to choose words carefully, "for two with the gift — no, that is wrong. It can be more than two." A very slight chuckle reached me in the dark. "Best to be precise."

We had spread our sleeping furs outdoors, for it was a fine night with no rain. "As I was saying, those with the gift can send themselves to another place. You know this. Any place that exists — and every place *does* exist, in potential. Infinite worlds, Yuzi." I heard only his breathing for a time. Even Hurasu, thousands of years old, was awed by things that were. "But suppose we send ourselves to exactly the same space, existing within each other?"

I could not even guess. It sounded messy and dangerous. "We can share our minds," he said. "Know one another's thoughts and knowledge. So had I hoped to do with Vasa. But that other has already done so. That was what damaged her." Was that anger? "He took what he wanted from her. Vasa probably does not even know this. She had no training to stand against it."

"And he is still there," I said. I could think of nothing else.

"Using her to keep an eye on things, I would guess. When I am ready, I will challenge him. I would hope to learn more first." A pause. "Exactly where he is, for one thing. None of what I could sense of that seemed right, but it seems connected to the gate you passed through."

I hesitated. Ah, why not? "Yuza said something much like that."

"Oh? Yuza was it? I knew I smelled a god. So they are uneasy too."

"You were coming to Nagi because of the gate, weren't you?" I asked. This suspicion had long been in my mind.

"Yes. I wanted to close it. When your group came through I wanted to all the more. The people of your world have become too advanced. They are a danger." Another soft chuckle. "Your rifle was not the first I had seen."

"I figured that was so," I replied. "The American?"

"Yes. I do not want more rifles here, Yuzi."

Neither did I. Hurasu went on. "The ways can not truly be closed or removed. They exist as part of the fabric of being. They can, however, be warded against entry. As the two from your world open only when great storms arise to power them, there is no point in attempting to hide them."

How they were 'warded' I could not imagine. Hurasu would explain if he saw fit. It was unlikely I would understand. "Then we should start south?" I asked. "To where we entered this world?"

"In time maybe. We should attend to things here first. Vasa."

"You can help her?" I was not positive he actually cared. His true concern was the gate and this other sorcerer he sensed.

"I hope so. She is a great talent, Yuzi. If she were not yours, I would steal her away to the other side of the world, train her in wizardry and make her my new Thun." I didn't have time to think that through before he went on. "That is dishonest. I apologize. I would make her my wife if I could."

After only meeting the girl? No, no, he had been aware of her for some time, and of her gift. I thought I understood. "You might have powerful offspring."

"Exactly. But she is better off here with you." I am not sure he believed that but it was nice to hear. "The gate — in theory," he went on, "I could ward it from the other side of the world. However, to do a proper job I need to wait until it opens again, and this I might not know unless I were near. I will go south and be ready when it happens. Even if it takes years of waiting."

"It is that important." This I stated; it was not a question.

"It is. But I fear it will not be so easy with this other, unseen one." His voice grew almost distant. "It is as if he is standing in the gate, seeing both directions."

"It is not possible to go back, is it?" All I had heard told me otherwise.

"No, it is one direction only. One of the very few ways between the worlds to be found where you were born. Here —" I could just see him wave an arm at our surroundings in the gloom. "Here there are many gates to other worlds. Most have been warded at some point against dangers."

"By you?"

"A few. Gods are responsible for some of it, I am sure. Many of them consider the gates their property and do not like trespassers." He laughed abruptly. "Considering some of the monsters that exist elsewhere, I do not care for them either."

I was ready to return to my search for sleep. But one more thing I had to ask. "You consider this world your property, don't you?"

Another laugh was what I had expected but Hurasu answered gravely. "Perhaps. Or perhaps like you, Yuzi, I take seriously my duty."

There was no more to be said that night.

45. Broken Spells

"Is Misi around?" I asked.

"Already back into the hills with the other hunters," said Anna. "He left with Tani at dawn." She did not look particularly upset that her husband was gone again. "The two of them sat up late as the boy told of his adventures."

"Enough adventures to last him for a lifetime, most likely." I took a seat beside her. "He'll be happy to stay home from now on."

"For some, that is enough. Tani has no ambitions for more." Anna laughed. "This place was made for him! Nothing to do but hunt, no one to tell him what to do."

"As long as he is not with you," I said. It was not polite maybe, but the woman laughed all the louder.

"He comes back anyway, now and then. One of the boys who went with you did not, I hear."

"Found himself a girl in the north. I think maybe Konosi did too." I wondered if he would return north with her eventually. I thought it likely.

"It will make him a better man," was Anna's opinion.

"He has already become a better man."

She nodded an agreement, slowly. Anna might not have liked him, perhaps still did not, but she was willing to admit this.

"Your Vasa is well?" she asked.

"Better than when I left."

Anna turned and looked at me intently for a moment. "So you see something is still wrong?"

"I do. He who came with me may be able to mend her."

"The wizard. Take care around him, Yuzi. I can see he is the sort who will have his own way." We sat silently a while. It was a fine morning. We both had things we should probably be doing. "Do you know what your way is yet?" she asked.

I could only shrug. "I will choose when it is time," I said. There were too many possibilities and not enough sureties to decide. Hurasu's business came first — and that only because of Vasa. What he did about his gate did not matter.

"I have had strange dreams," said Anna. It seemed an odd change of subject. "I have seen a great ruler of some sort. I could not make out his face. Who knows? Maybe it is you, my tsar." She gave me a slightly weary smile.

To that I shook my head. "Let others rule. Even being a hetman is too much work!" We both laughed at that, and I rose, nodding a farewell. I should go see Vasa.

Hurasu was again with her, and Ati. The latter turned to me as I entered his house. "I like the young shaman you brought home with you, Yuzi," he said at once. "Do you think she will stay?"

"Only if Konosi does," I quipped. I had no idea if it were true. Maybe she would be willing to live by the sea with him. Maybe they would return to her home in the north. Maybe they would fight and not be together at all.

Hurasu seemed to be engaging with Vasa in some manner. Both sat calmly, eyes half-closed. "They've been at that quite some time." Ati sounded slightly concerned. Suddenly Hurasu's eyes came wide open.

Simultaneously, Vasa seemed to faint, slowly sinking to one side. The sorcerer caught her and lowered her carefully to lie on a bed of furs. "I fear I have revealed myself," he said. He did not sound as though he feared anything. He glanced at the girl, seemingly sound asleep. "Vasa is free. It was best I did this. I thought upon it much after, ah, exploring yesterday."

He rose. "And we must depart for the south at once."

It would take time to gather men, supplies. "It is a long trek," I said. And there were hostile trolls along the way.

"No, we will go by boat. A few men only. That is all we need if we get there swiftly."

Best recruit some of them at the village by the bay, maybe, where our boats rested. "I'll get things together," I promised, and hastened out the doorway. To whom should I talk? For a moment I was bewildered by the suddenness of this new plan. Konosi, maybe. Where was he?

I need but ask. The whole village knew, I think! I found him with Ashaga and her brother, eating with Olga. He looked up at me, giving a friendly grin. "Did you know this one," he asked, gesturing toward the priestess, "is going to allow her innocent daughter to marry our Yeli?" Daniel? What did Leni think of that? Ah, not now.

"We are leaving again," I said. "We must go to the place where we entered this world." I almost forgot to add, "Oh, by boat."

"I shall come, of course," said Konosi. He gave the two northerners a questioning look.

I spoke before anyone else had a chance. "Ashaga, I ask you to stay and look after Vasa." She nodded but obviously wanted to come along. "And I would as soon you stay and look after Ashaga," I said to her brother. "This is not your problem."

"Then why am I here?" Tashi gave me a lopsided smile. "Besides, I want to see more of the coast."

"We three only, then," I said, "and Hurasu. If we need more, we'll find them at the coast.

We left before noon and traveled into the night. Our provisions were minimal. We could get more at the bay. It was hard to keep up with Hurasu; he would not walk but jogged forward steadily, untiringly, over the heather-clad hills. He seemed driven by his need to arrive at the gate as soon as possible, but offered no explanation.

We had no breath to ask! We were come to that time of year when the sunlight lingered late; too, the southern lights were playing along the horizon. We could see them glimmering faintly on the dark rolling waters of the bay when we arrived.

There was hospitality, a meal, an explanation, a couple hours of sleep. Then, two hide-covered boats slipped into the water, raised sails, and headed into the dawn.

46. An Opening

Mazi had come with us. Five men only, he with Konosi, Hurasu and I with Tashi. Mazi had no knowledge of sails but received an education on this trip.

We would undoubtedly make better time this way than by walking. The winds were with us. That would not matter so much on the way back, I assumed. Hurasu would do what he needed to do and that would be that. It was but wishful thinking and I knew it at the time. Things go wrong.

First, a long stretch of coast running southeastward. This was familiar to Mazi, the favored shores for fishing and for hunting seals. It looked far more inviting than the rugged cliffs north of the bay — yet the lands were just as empty. As soon as we were on our way, sails filled and no need to paddle, Hurasu sat and spoke to someone from afar. "Ati," he announced when done. "Vasa is awake and seems herself again." The sorcerer sounded as if he expected as much.

"I never thanked you, in all the hurry of getting away," I said. "So I do so now." Even if it were for reasons of his own.

He might have suspected my thoughts. "It was not right to leave her so," he said. "I hope to deal with he who was responsible."

I did not care about that. It was over and this sorcerer he and the others could not see could remain unseen permanently. If Hurasu did his warding of the gate, maybe that would be an end to him.

The sorcerer spoke to others from afar as we sailed along too. He checked in with his realm on the other side of the world, and with some shaman he knew, one who lived near but not in his kingdom. "I think I shall visit him and other old friends when done here," he told me. "And ward the other gate, which lies near their home." He regarded me for a few seconds with his dark eyes. "You could come to my home if you wish. Otherwise, I travel halfway around the world by myself." It was quite an offer. But could Vasa make such a journey?

Within three days we had rounded a point and saw a wide bay spread before us. "Our camping place," Konosi called to me from the other boat. So it was, the place where we stayed the longest on the journey north, the place Mug and Leni had come to us. One could live there, I thought, but would probably have no reason to. We passed by and, eventually, the shoreline began to curve back to the south and then the southwest. I knew what to look for, the smaller bay where we had first camped, where we had first come to the sea. We would walk from there.

I hoped no new bear had moved into the neighborhood. There would be seals; indeed, they might make landing the boats difficult.

The seas were rough. They are always rough around Nagi. We passed through small squalls now and then, and spied icebergs more than once to remind us we were near an arctic region. Or should I say antarctic? I neither knew nor particularly cared. The ice was out in the deeper sea and floating into that great watery expanse of which Hurasu had told. Konosi and I recognized our destination almost simultaneously.

I think mating season had passed. The seals lay languidly on the gray sand and ignored the men hauling their boats ashore. We ignored them equally. Which way to the gate, to the spot where we had walked into the wonder of a new and very empty land? I could vaguely guess and Konosi was no better. We had not been noting landmarks at the time. This land was notably empty of landmarks.

No need. Hurasu immediately strode off in the direction he chose. "I must tell you what I know, now," he said, as we caught up with him. "I saw this other. I spoke to him. It was unavoidable."

"A sorcerer like you," I said.

"So he is. He named himself Xahun. That is not a name but a title; it means 'lord' in the world in which I was born." This Xahun, then, came also from Hurasu's world. From Atlantis, if we were to believe that. And he, too, had strayed into my own earth.

"He is in Russia," Hurasu went on. "Somehow, he found a way to partially open the gate and seek through it. It would be near impossible for even the most powerful sorcerer to send himself out from your world normally. It is simply too closed off from magic." A low, harsh laugh. "I was never able too, anyway. If the gate truly opens, however it is accomplished, he will come through."

He sighed. "But that will give me the opportunity to ward it permanently. Worth the price, perhaps." The sorcerer looked about. "We are there. Now we can but wait."

It looked like the right place. The sea was distant but still visible; I remembered that. Probably any of a number of other places here looked much the same. All that day we waited and through the night, in a cold camp. I felt exposed there, remembering the savage trolls that dwelt not so far away.

Hurasu shook me awake in a cold clear dawn. "It happens," he said. I aroused the others, as the sorcerer stood staring across the empty lands. Was there something there? A swimming of the air, a darkening. Like a cave.

Yes, a cave that seemed to open out of nothing, from a wall of air. Out of that cave rumbled a tank, a red star painted prominently on its turret.

Part 4. The Gate

47. Invaders

A column of soldiers followed the tank. Hurasu fell flat on the ground. "Hide yourselves," he hissed. The heather and sedge were high enough to give concealment.

The sorcerer seemed to have immediately gone into some sort of trance. He was doing what he needed to do, what he had come to do, I assumed. I remembered my monocular and pulled it out, trained it on my fellow countrymen, this contingent of the Red Army, that had just come from seemingly nowhere. The men were looking about, confused, but maintained order. I looked to the tank. There was a man, an officer I would assume, standing on the front deck, one hand resting on the cannon. I focused. Yes, an officer, a dark haired man with a mustache, and skin the color of old parchment.

This was surely the man who had harmed Vasa. I wished I had my Mosin Nagant and its one remaining cartridge with me at that moment. I heard distant cries. The cave had disappeared, perhaps before all came through who were intended to come through. I turned the scope back to the leader. There was anger on his face. Then, of a sudden it turned to laughter. He was here; that was probably all that really mattered to this Xahun.

"Let's get out of here," whispered Hurasu, back with us. "I did what I intended and there is no way we can deal with those who came through. Not now." A grim smile. "No others will follow, now or ever."

If we stayed close to the ground and kept the low rolling hills between ourselves and the soldiers, we might escape detection. Long enough, anyway. Ah, I was thinking like a man of this land. Those soldiers over there had rifles. They could kill us at a distance.

Did their leader know we were somewhere near? Hurasu had said he could work his — what should I call it? Magic? He could work his magic from anywhere. For all Xahun knew, he could be far away. I did not know what he and the soldiers were up to. Keeping myself hidden meant that I could not see them either, and I would not chance discovery.

"This is not the way to the boats," whispered Tashi. We were so far away there was no need to whisper.

"Best to get as far from those — those invaders as we can, first," I said. "We can circle back to the bay."

When we came to a good hidden spot behind a rocky outcrop, I felt safe again taking a look. It was too far to tell much, even through my glass. I could not make out individual features at this distance, but I could see they were not moving yet.

"What was that thing my enemy rode upon?" asked Hurasu. "It is mechanical, is it not?"

"Yes," said Konosi. "A tank. It carries a very large rifle."

"I knew the people of your world were clever about such things. Malvern — the man from America — told me much of what they had invented since I lived there. Machines that fly, even."

I was glad none of those had been brought through. Perhaps they would have been, given time. "I am more concerned about the many small rifles those soldier carry," I said. "The tank requires fuel and I doubt they have enough for it to travel far."

Hurasu nodded. "That is good to know." His eyes went to the distant men, though naught could be made out from here. "Were I their leader, I would take this tank to a good camp and leave it there as a weapon of defense."

That made considerable sense. "So they will reconnoiter first," I guessed, "and find a likely spot from which to operate. Who can know what plans they might have beyond that?"

"The men who sent them may have intended conquest. He who leads them now may not care about that," the sorcerer said. "Let us get to our boats. It would be best to sail at once." He stopped suddenly. "Xahun is attempting to speak to me. This I shall not do, not now."

At once, my own thoughts went to Vasa. Could this hidden sorcerer who was hidden no more again enter her mind? He was in our own world now, with no barriers save the girl's own ability to reject him. But Hurasu had broken the bond Xahun had created. Maybe she would be safe. And what of all the other shamans? What of all those with the gifts of sorcery throughout this world?

What of Ati and Ashaga? Hurasu was right. We should return to them at once. We could safely stand now, and jogged toward the sea. "Our return trip will not as easy," spoke Tashi. "The northeasterly winds yet prevail." There was nothing to done about that. If we must paddle all the way home, hundreds of kilometers, so be it.

"I will not attempt to communicate with anyone from afar for some time," Hurasu was saying. "It might reveal me too soon."

"Won't you be safe once we are at sea?" asked Konosi.

"It is not my safety that concerns me. I would not want this Xahun to know we have spied his arrival. Not yet."

The day was dimming by the time we reached the beach but we chose to launch immediately, into the long twilight of summer. The winds were against us, it was true. At least they should not drive us onto the rocky coast! We paddled all the night. I still had the compass I had brought with me from the other world, Red Army issue. With that we were able to keep ourselves headed somewhat in the proper direction through a dark turbulent sea.

In the days that followed we paddled on, keeping the coast in sight. Sometimes the sails were usable; sometimes they were not. There was much time to think. This Xahun would have known the gate went only one way. If the Soviet government — maybe all the way to Stalin — or the Red Army had backed his adventure, he might not have told them of this. Those soldiers of Russia were as now thoroughly divided from their home as I. What could they do? Whom could they serve but the man who led them here?

Xahun was probably pleased that the gate was now closed and warded, and no one from the other side could interfere. He might have done so himself, given time. He might also have brought through a much larger force first. It was good that was prevented.

So I worked things out in my head, as we worked our way slowly north. I might have been completely wrong. At last we paddled into the great bay by which my people had once camped, and here we put in to the shore. I thought of this as a halfway point. It was not exactly so; this I knew but I thought of it so anyway. Both Tashi and Konosi felt the sailing would be easier once we rounded the point on its north side and slid northwesterly toward home.

Here Hurasu at last broke his silence, sending himself out to speak from afar.

48. In the Air

"Xahun undoubtedly noticed," spoke Hurasu. "It does not matter." He had gone 'away' several times, speaking to others, over the space of an hour or so. To me, he said, "Your troll friends are home safely, with Vuk's new wife. A lovely girl, as seen through his eyes." The sorcerer smiled at his little jest. "He felt Xahun's presence, as did his master. I do not think they want to get involved in our dealings with him."

I couldn't blame them. "Many have felt that presence," he went on, "throughout Nagi and throughout the world. He is not attempting to hide himself."

"You do," I said. It seemed that way to me.

"Yes, I have always. There is no reason to attract attention." A man after my own heart was Hurasu. "Vasa is well," he said now. "Quite recovered, it seems. I even spoke with her a little. We must have a longer conversation when we are together again."

All this was good. But — "Then this sorcerer may know where you are?"

"He might have some idea. Almost certainly he learned nothing from me but some of those to whom I spoke are not so well guarded." He shrugged. "It matters not now. We are too far away for him to touch us."

"So we sail on?" asked Mazi. "I'd just as soon get home."

"We sail on," agreed the sorcerer.

First we slaughtered a seal to provide fresh meat. Our stores were low. This delayed us the better part of a day. Then a launch in the early light and up and around the point to the north, into Mazi's familiar waters, along his familiar coast. The winds were good.

I heard, near noon, an odd buzzing, faint, distant. It sounded like nothing I had heard in this world. Ah, Hurasu had noted it too and was scanning the open seas around us. It grew stronger. It grew familiar. I looked toward the skies. There, on our southern horizon, gaining quickly. The invading force *had* brought an airplane, most likely one that could be dismantled for easy transport.

A small and simple monoplane, with a rectangular high wing and open cockpit, I could see as it closed the distance. Xahun could touch us, after all. I hoped it was scouting only. We would be defenseless if it carried a gun. The aircraft came low, circled us. One man peered out through goggles. I could see no machine gun mounted anywhere. It was too small and light for that sort of thing, surely.

Not too small and light for its pilot to hold an automatic rifle. An old Federov maybe. They had not been in service for years but we Red Army men had all heard there were many in storage. It was still a heavy and clumsy weapon for a pilot to aim out the side of his cockpit. The first burst of fire came nowhere close, churning the water well ahead of our boats. He clearly had orders to kill us if he could. Or to kill Hurasu. The rest of us were only collateral.

He might become lucky if he kept at it. There was nothing any of us could do. No, not even our great sorcerer. Maybe given time he could pull something from another world as had the unfortunate Thun. Something as simple as a fog to hide us. No, the wind would carry that away too quickly. The plane turned, flat and low, for another pass. I could see details of the craft, the small radial engine, five cylinders, and the sturdy plank-like bracing below the thick wing. It would be very slow, I thought. It must have taken a long time to get here. He had to fly to the side of us to get a shot, his automatic rifle firing across his body, to his left.

Something beyond him. Another airplane? Surely not. It was hard to make out but clearly speeding directly toward us. Then I could not see it at all, for the aircraft was blocking it, the pilot spraying bullets toward us. Some whistled close but none of us were hit. The only holes in our skin-covered boat were safely above the water line.

Then the plane suddenly careened, slipping sideways in the air, spinning. The wing detached from the body as both plummeted into the sea. Hovering where it had flown only seconds before was a slender winged shape. A dragon.

"We should see to the pilot," called Konosi. He was right. We should not let the man drown if he had survived his crash. And he might be valuable in some way. So might his gun if it had not gone to the bottom. The dragon hovered a moment more, eyeing us, and then flitted away toward land. Why had it done this, rescued us? Did it simply see the airplane as an intruder in its territory? We paddled to the wreckage. No machine gun. But the pilot was quite alive and had a handgun. We could use that, maybe.

He was hauled aboard Konosi's boat. His uniform gave the man a rank of starshina. A year ago, my ambition had been to wear that uniform, hadn't it? That Josef Dobrov seemed a very different man from who I was now. Ah well, nothing to do but continue our journey home. It was most unlikely there was even one more airplane in this world.

I could see Konosi conversing with our prisoner, as he tended his sail. Mazi sat and scowled at the man, and occasionally dipped his paddle to aid in steering. Maybe the priest could get something from him. I would wait until we reached our port before bothering with this soldier. "You have dealt with dragons before," said Hurasu, after some time. "I could see this."

"Not so closely. Why did he fly away after the attack?"

"She. It was a female dragon. I do not know, nor do I understand why she came to our aid. Had she remained a while, I might have tried to talk with her."

That somewhat astounded me. "They can speak?" I thought them only brutes, wild animals.

"Dragons are as intelligent as men. Maybe more intelligent. They have a rich language, one all dragons speak."

I considered this fact. Dragon populations all around the world would have to keep in contact for that to remain so. They must travel a great deal. "Perhaps we shall find out then, some day."

"Perhaps," he agreed.

49. Goddesses

Sergey was bewildered. He had not realized he was in a new world. He had thought it was Siberia and the Red Army had discovered a new method of quickly moving troops. That was the official word that had been handed down to the starshina before the secret operation had begun in the Urals.

"What then, did you think this sea was?" asked Konosi. We stood on the shore of our own bay, nearly home at last.

"At first, maybe the Caspian," the man said. "Then I thought maybe we had been transported to the Arctic, somehow. It is best not to question too much."

A sentiment I could share. Or did once. Sergey was completely harmless now, with no gun and his people hundreds of kilometers distant. There was no need to guard him. He could do nothing. And he even apologized for shooting at us. "It was ordered by the captain," he said. "I only obeyed."

"No harm done," Konosi told him. He was a squat fellow, strongly built, with features that hinted of Asians somewhere among his ancestors. Therefor, he looked much like the people here.

"I still do not understand why I suddenly lost control of the airplane," he said. "Its structure should not have failed. I assembled it myself!"

"Oh, a, um, bird hit it," I told him. I didn't know if he could quite accept a dragon attack. "An extremely large bird."

"Ah!" That seemed to satisfy him. "Had I not been wrestling with that damned gun, I might have been able to regain control."

We had set about teaching him our language almost as soon as he had been pulled into Konosi's boat, but he was a slow learner. He didn't seem to see a point to it. Sergey did not quite understand yet that he would never return to Russia.

He was, however, entirely willing to believe our claim that his leader was a traitor who had misled the generals or the party or whoever had approved his project. He did not like the captain at all. "He did not even seem Russian," he said. That, for him, was reason enough to distrust anyone. "And that name, Zahunsky. Captain Zahunsky. Who ever heard of such a name? Not I, Comrades."

We could only agree. "We go on tomorrow to our village," I told the starshina. "You can come along or remain here. It does not matter much."

He looked to Konosi. "Are you going too?" The priest nodded. "Then no one left here that speaks Russian. I'd better go with you. I like Mazi, though. He's important here, right?"

"He is," agreed Konosi. "One of the leaders of the men of the sea. If you stay, he could teach you the language."

Sergey was having none of that. He and Konosi wandered off somewhere, still conversing, but I stayed there, on the slope above the bay. It was a good warm night — as nights go on Nagi — and I could see no reason to close myself in one of the stone houses. I could sleep right here, and in the morning be on my way to Vasa. Beyond that? Who could say? I supposed we would have to deal with Xahun eventually but he was far away now.

Wasn't he really Hurasu's problem, anyway? A rival sorcerer, come to challenge him. I lay back, staring at the sky. There were few clouds. I doubted it would rain on me in the night.

"There is the man. We are disturbing his sleep." I recognized the voice.

"We are goddesses. Who is he to complain?" Another female voice. That one I did not know, though the two seemed much alike. I sat up. Yuza stood there, much as before. The woman beside her was was almost as tall and looked very like the goddess. A pair of shaggy but shapely hounds flanked her trouser-clad legs. Those were shapely too.

"This is my sister Beyana," said Yuza. "You needn't ogle her. She doesn't like men."

"Maybe if I found one who could keep up with me," sniffed the other goddess.

"Better to stay ahead of them," returned Yuza. She shifted her attention back to me. "So the hidden wizard has revealed himself."

"So he has. But Hurasu closed and locked the door behind him." That was what had truly worried her, wasn't it? Her and whatever other gods had taken interest.

"That is so, and well done," said Beyana. I think maybe she considered Hurasu a man who might be able to keep up with her. "But there is still this other. What does he name himself?"

"Xahun," I answered.

"Yes. He is not a good man."

"But a mortal," her sister reminded her. "He will go in time."

Beyana frowned. "But what harm might he do to my people before then?"

"*Your* people, Sister?" laughed Yuza.

"The people of the forests and wild places," said Beyana. "Both those who speak and those who do not. I fear for them when one such as this Xahun holds sway."

I was, as to be expected, leery of interrupting a pair of goddesses, but they were taking much time to get to anything. "Are there other gods who are concerned, my ladies?" I asked.

Beyana spoke gravely. "Some of them do not care. Some, I think, are afraid. Yes, even gods can fear."

"Most felt I should take care of it all, since I have already taken a look at things," said Yuza. "But my sister is right, there is fear. Xahun is the sort who would disrupt many worlds in his quest for power, even those of the gods."

"We have heard of no man doing what he did at the gate, forcing it open as he did. Nowhere may be safe from him."

Apparently old-fashioned smiting did not work. Despite their tricks, despite their apparent immortality, these gods might be less powerful than the great wizards. "Then it is his knowledge you fear, as much as the man." I was about to go on with this line of thought, when I noted the goddesses looking beyond me. Yuza beckoned to someone.

It was Hurasu. Maybe he had smelled gods again. "Sit, mortal," spoke Beyana, "and listen to our tale." The words may have been of command but there always seemed to be a laugh behind what the goddess said. That might have been true of both sisters. Hurasu took a place beside me without a word.

"There was a world once, a beautiful world," began Yuza.

Beyana interrupted. "Do not be long-winded, Sister. You knew the world well, Hurasu. Know you any of what occurred after you left?"

"I do not," he said, evenly.

"Know then that it now lies in ruins. Men like Xahun destroyed it."

"And he escaped to do the same elsewhere," added Yuza. "He escaped by the same way between worlds that you traveled."

"Men became too powerful for their own good in Atlantis," Beyana stated. I do not think Yuza quite shared her sister's opinion but she did not choose to argue against it.

Hurasu sighed. "I wish that I had not learned this. Yet it does not surprise me. How long was this Xahun in that other world?" He turned his head slightly toward me. "Yuzi's world."

"A century or two?" This was Yuza asking Beyana.

"No more than that," said her sister. "Not as long as you lingered, Lord Hurasu. But he had learned much gate lore and knew what to seek."

Again, knowledge. This, as much as anything, was Xahun's sin in their eyes. But I was also entirely willing to believe he was truly evil. All his actions so far corroborated that.

"It would be best he died here," spoke Beyana. "His wards are too strong for us to get close. Maybe if I could get within bow shot —"

"I doubt it would work," Hurasu said. "Nor am I sure I could defeat him in a battle of magic, a battle of our wills. Never have I had to admit that about any man in the last two thousand years."

"What about a bullet?" I asked.

"It should make him as dead as any other mortal. As would my steel through his body." He laughed. "He is unlikely to make himself available for either."

"All the shamans and sorcerers of this land will aid you," said Beyana, her voice now low and steady. "All of this world, maybe."

Her sister was not of the same mind. "There are always those who will throw in with one such as Xahun. He might offer them power. They might be jealous of Hurasu. This is true of ordinary mortals, too, not just those who deal in magic. Be careful of traitors, both of you," she warned us. "We will help as we can. Beyana and I are watching." With that, ropes

165

of smoke coiled about them and both disappeared.

"You have picked a good spot to sleep," remarked Hurasu, and lay himself down.

50. Marriages

"I sensed another in your mind, one you did not know was there," Hurasu told Vasa.

She nodded. "I can see now where he was. Why was it hidden before?"

The sorcerer thought a moment before answering. "Not hidden. You simply did not know where to look. I can teach you this." He glanced toward old Ati. "You have already learned much from your master."

The shaman lifted a shaggy white eyebrow. "It is kind of you to say so."

"It is only truth. Vasa would be mad or dead now had you not prepared her." Hurasu turned back to the woman. She looked much better now, I had to admit. Healthier than when I had left her. Maybe healthier than ever she had looked, and more confident. "Xahun may grow interested in you now. He threw you aside before, as of no consequence."

The words of Yuza came back to me, her warnings of temptation, of traitors. This powerful enemy of ours — yes, ours, and not just Hurasu's — could offer Vasa much. He might attempt to seduce her, and would not have the ethical restraints Hurasu had shown. Not that I completely trusted him either.

"Then she should learn more, so she may defend herself," I said.

The fifth person there, Ashaga, spoke. "I would not mind learning more myself. I was only an apprentice to Katira and not that far along."

"You learned much from your father, before ever you went to your mistress at Prazim," said Ati. "I could see this. You will be a good shaman — wherever you choose to settle." I think maybe he expected to lose Vasa and was seeking another to replace him here. I could not really see Ashaga taking on that role.

"We must send messages to all the shamans of Nagi," said Hurasu, "or as many as possible. It would be easier to send elementals than to attempt to speak with each."

Ati nodded. "That would be fatiguing."

"And take too much time. You deal with elementals?"

"The Ihe? I have," the shaman replied, "but not often."

Hurasu took this without expression. "Very well. Let us make a beginning of it." He looked from the old shaman to the rest of us. "No need for you to stay. We will not have time to explain what we are doing." A dismissal.

"May I stay and watch?" asked Vasa. Hurasu only nodded.

Ashaga saw no reason to remain and observe something she did not understand and would not be a part of. She and I stepped out into the morning. "Konosi was happy to return to you," I said.

"And I was happy to have him back," came the girl's reply. She sounded a little frustrated "But he still refuses to sleep with me. I do not understand it!"

Ah. I should have suspected. "It comes from being a priest. He believes he should wait until you marry." This was certainly true — in part. It was also likely he had many doubts.

"Then we must get married soon!" she decided.

Indeed. And then? Would they remain? None of that mattered so much; we had other concerns now. "There may be many weddings soon," was all I said. Vasa and I? Yeli and Telpata, the daughter of Leni and Olga?

"I wish my brother were here," said Ashaga. Tashi chose to remain by the bay, ostensibly to repair the boats. I think he preferred the company of the men of the sea. He was one who definitely would not remain in the south but, having once made the voyage, might return at times.

I spied a clump of people. "There is your intended husband," I said. Yeli was there too, and Anna. In fact, I realized, all of them were Russians, some of those whom I had led here. In their middle stood Sergey.

"No, no," the starshina was saying. "He is not a good man." Voices rose, too many at once, all in Russian.

"What are they saying?" asked Ashaga.

"They are talking about Xahun." The arrival of more of their countrymen surely was something to be excited about. I did not even think of those soldiers as my countrymen anymore. This was my place, not Russia. But others would not let go of the old so easily. Some were not happy with their lives here.

"But he sounds like a man of power." Anna's voice rose over the others. "A man who comes to conquer." Did she approve of that? Was she remembering the dream of which she had told me?

"Maybe he could lead us home," someone said.

It was time I said something, before this went further. "No one can go home," I told them. "It has always been only one way. This Xahun knew this and fooled his superiors, letting them think their soldiers could come and go. Now all are trapped here, his to command."

This did not seem to bother some. "So he comes to rule," I heard, and, "Craftiness is desirable in a leader." Some of these men and women were too Russian yet, too inclined to admire the authoritarian. Some would never change.

"Men like him are the reason many of us were on our way to the Gulag," came Yeli's voice above the rest. It sounded clearer and more confident than ever I remembered. There was none of his habitual mockery in it.

"I thought it was because I knifed my wife's lover," said someone, to laughs all around.

I laughed with them, not because it was so funny but to show I remained one of them. "You have mobbed poor Sergey long enough," I announced. "Let us get him somewhere to rest a while."

There were some grumbles but I was able to lead the soldier away. I think maybe he was happy to be rescued. Yeli and Konosi followed; I thought for a moment Anna would too, but she seemed to change her mind and turned the other way.

"You are a politician," observed the starshina. It was true, unfortunately. I had been made into one. Then, "It is so, then, that I shall never leave this place? My men, too?"

"It is." There was nothing more to say than that.

"Then I suppose I had best learn the language after all."

"We are the ones to teach you, Sergi," said Yeli. He had already changed the man's name to one in the form of his adopted people. He looked about the village and slowly smiled. "It is a good place. I thought I did not belong when first we came, that I would always be an outsider, would wish to leave." His eyes went to me for a second or two. He had thought we two would move along, hadn't he? "But I am accepted here, accepted as a poet. A bard. And soon to be accepted as a husband."

"There is enough work for a poet?" I think Sergi meant it jokingly.

"There is enough work for me to be useful and a poet at once." He held his hands before him, palms up. "I have learned to use these."

Konosi chuckled. "He thinks he is Tolstoy."

Yeli slowly shook his head, a half-smile on his lips. "It is enough," he said, "to no longer be Daniel Erlich and become Yeli."

51. Sahra

The ihes, the elementals, as Ashaga explained it to us, were beings bound to no one world. Therefor, they were invisible to most of us. "They are rather mindless," she said, "but they can carry messages anywhere. Some of them can and some of them will."

"Messages to anyone?" I asked.

"Oh, no, only to other shamans or wizards," she said. "No, I do not put that correctly. They could carry messages to anyone but anyone could not hear them." The girl gave her typical little frown, two tiny lines above her nose. "Some say they are related to the gods, who can also move from world to world. All others are bound to one realm."

"Unless they came through a gate," added Vasa. She had said little up to then. "Hurasu taught me this. Gates break all bonds to a world." One of her silly giggles erupted. I had greatly missed hearing them. "Otherwise, we Russians would all have popped back home eventually!"

That was useless information, truly. None of us were likely to go to another world again, whether through a gate or not. But I suppose it is good to know things.

"Ita and Herasu sent messages all over," continued Vasa. "Most shamans were not willing to get involved with any of this right now. Still, it is right that they were informed." She nodded her head firmly in approval of her own words, before adding, "The trolls want nothing to do with Xahun!"

That did not surprise me. I doubted it surprised Hurasu either. Out of nothing more than curiosity, I asked, "Did they send word to the goblins?"

Vasa knew nothing of goblins. It was Ashaga who said, "I think they are always aware of what is going on. They and all the fay."

"There are other fay here?" That could be good to know, too.

"Some ogres, for sure," said the girl. "I'm not sure about any others. There are said to be High Fay on the mainland. Or —" She thought on her next words before letting them go. "Or gates by which they can come and go to their own worlds."

I had heard some mention of the High Fay, mostly in songs. They seemed to be what we thought of as elves or fairies in the old world. Again, of no use now, and maybe never.

"Oh!" Vasa suddenly sat up straight, her eyes staring forward. She shook her head a couple times, then relaxed, her body slumping forward before she caught herself. "That was our enemy. He tried to ensnare me again."

"We must tell Hurasu!" Ashaga said at once.

Vasa held up a hand. "No, he knows of this. It is not the first time Xahun has tested me this day. If I do not let him in, I am safe." Had I any doubt of the need to destroy the sorcerer, it disappeared at that moment.

"I suspect he will grow tired of trying," she continued. "He has other things to do."

"He could be marching north. Would that we could know, and know where he sets up his base."

"This Xahun probably wishes he knew things, too," replied Ashaga. "You blinded him by destroying his flying device." That was so. I had not thought it through, only being thankful we had not been shot!

Konosi beamed. He had been too busy stuffing himself with roasted rabbit to say much before. "Ashaga is bright. She sees the meanings of things."

"Wasted on you," was Yeli's opinion. Yes, he could certainly still be sarcastic.

"As is poor young Telpata," responded the priest. "I know not what the girl sees in you."

"All women are wasted on men," the young shaman informed them. "But what else are we to do?" The look she and Konosi exchanged answered quite clearly 'nothing.'

Vasa was looking beyond her. "Hurasu comes," she announced. The sorcerer strolled, seemingly with no cares nor hurry, in our direction.

"Anything left?" he asked, casually taking a place in our circle. Between the girls, I noted. "Ah, that will do." He took a chunk of reindeer meat, bit off a piece, and sat chewing for a while. "Yuzi," he said, "you and I must take a short trip. Just we two."

"When?"

"Now." He rose. "Come." Hurasu started off, still holding his chunk of meat, and taking bites from it. I shrugged, nodded a goodbye, and followed. We walked from the village toward the northwest, perhaps a couple kilometers. It looked no different there than elsewhere.

The sorcerer called out in a language I had never heard before. Like no other was it; it sounded not even human. Down the slope wound a long lithe figure. It sat up, at a short distance, and answered in the same tongue. Very well. So dragons could, indeed, speak.

Hurasu turned to me. "This young lady's name is quite long and quite unpronounceable, even for me. She says to call her Sahra." That meant nothing more nor less than 'sister' in the language of Nagi. I assumed the dragon knew this. "She can understand you, some," Hurasu went on, "but she is not able to voice human words."

Half of me wanted to run away but the other half remembered his manners. "I greet you, Sahra," I said, giving her a bow.

"Well done," whispered Hurasu. "Sahra came to see me early this morning and explained some things."

"She is the one who saved us?"

"She is. And you saved her, once." The dragon seemed to be following this.

"Ah! The one I fed last winter. She was welcome to it, with no obligations."

Hurasu chuckled. "Dragons always feel obligations. It is their nature." A string of incomprehensible guttural growlings came from Sahra. "She truly believes your generosity saved her life that day." He looked up as more dragon talk was directed at us. "You and your companion, who continued to provide for her a while after you left."

"A good man," I said. I was glad he had done so. "So her obligation has been fulfilled and I thank her."

"Not necessarily. She feels there is a bond." He turned to me. "She considers you her friend, simply put. It is rare a dragon will do so."

"Then I accept this. I shall be your friend too, my lady," I called to her. Maybe she understood, but Hurasu translated as well. Then they carried on a more extended conversation. At last, Sahra spread her wings, gave me a last lingering gaze and launched into the overcast skies. I watched her slowly beat her way upward. Flying would not be so easy for such large creatures.

"It was not for you she came to me, interrupting my morning bath. Not only for you." We started back toward the village. "Her kind, too, are bothered by this invasion. And they very much disliked the idea of men flying!"

I could imagine. "So," he went on, "they are offering some help. Not much. Dragons remain dragons and they are rather selfish creatures. But Sahra says they will keep an eye on Xahun for us."

"That would be useful." Rather an obvious statement, I realized.

"It would. Sahra herself might be willing to give us a little more than that, thanks to you." He seemed to be fighting an urge to grin. "She is quite a young girl, as dragons go. I think she may have a bit of a crush on you."

52. Trouble With Trolls

The ordinary people of the village, and those villages around it, were as difficult to rouse as the shamans of the trolls. This Xahun was far away. What concerns was he of theirs?

Perhaps tribes further south might see it differently, but it seemed likely the invaders would turn our way. The dragons confirmed that a couple days later. The force, tank and all, was slowly rolling north. In time, they would impinge on the reindeer pastures; then we would see if attitudes changed.

"I think the ordinary troll folk would be more likely to assist than their shamans," I told Hurasu. "They are more jealous of their territories and less trusting of outsiders." Especially those savage trolls of the south. Would Xahun's little army have encountered them yet?

All those guns would probably make short work of any attacking trolls. How many guns? How much ammunition? They too would run out eventually. I had handed over my last round to Ivan. He carried his Mosin Nagant still, now with a full magazine — the five shots remaining to us. The other two rifles were useless without cartridges. Ha, maybe we could liberate some!

Hurasu had been considering what I said. "Then let us visit these trolls," he decided. "If some are willing, we could scout south and maybe see what our enemy is up to. The dragons see but there is much they do not understand."

"Mug is probably the man to see. The troll to see. I think he and many of his tribe are with the reindeer herds in the south."

"I will speak afar to Vuk," he said. "And he to his master. Zup, is it not?" I nodded. "I would wish both of them to be at our meeting."

That was arranged by the evening. We would meet in the hills and talk of things. After that, who could say? No one much was interested in going with the two of us until I mentioned it to Sergi. "You would have time to teach me more of your language as we travel," he said. "Everyone here is too busy and I know not what to do with myself. I would see more of this country too."

Alright with me. Hurasu approved; indeed, he thought the starshina might be able to provide some insights on the soldiers with whom he had arrived. Then Yeli asked to come along. He too was a bit tired of the village.

Yeli was not much suited to herding, though, as most of the men, he helped at times. Nor was he a hunter by nature. He had made himself useful by mastering crafts, and especially the working of stone. No, not building stones — I mean the flint blades and points that were such important tools for these people.

"My work is still crude," he claimed. "It might take a lifetime to master. But I am willing to take a lifetime." His voice was firm but I think maybe his eyes dreamed. "A peaceful lifetime here with Telpata."

How the man had changed! He would have lived and died in misery in Russia, in and out of the work camps, never finding what he sought. And Telpata would be good for him. She was a robust young lady of perhaps eighteen. Telpata would keep Yeli in line, I was sure.

As Ashaga would Konosi. "Ashaga is much like you," he had once said. Too much like me, I thought. Both Ashaga and Telpata were better paired with the dreamers they had chosen. And I — I had my own dreamer.

Vasa would never have survived the camps. That is certain. For that, above all other reasons, I was thankful we had found another world.

Three days we walked south and a little west of south, toward that cave in the hills where once our people had slept. It was a good place to meet, central to all. Mug was there, and Zup and Vuk, and a handful of other notable trolls. Leni had tagged along too.

These trolls were skeptical of our ideas. "We have not been bothered," said one. "Why stir up a powerful sorcerer?"

"He is already astir," stated Hurasu, "as am I." It didn't hurt to remind the troll shamans he was also far more powerful than any of them. "Xahun will not stay where he is. He desires to rule over this world."

"But we are poor trolls," objected Mug. "Surely he will go on north and seek a kingdom there." The troll might be right about that. Nagi would make a poor base for Xahun, and certainly no place to recruit a conquering army. Were Hurasu not here he might go right past all of us.

"I suspect Xahun will find that is true of much of this world," laughed Hurasu. The laugh was short, curt. "It is still primitive and sparsely settled. He will be disappointed and then — then he will think of building an army here to conquer other worlds. It is his way. So he did in Yuzi's world. So will he do here, and throw you into a great war across worlds. I can see the ruins of this land when he is done."

There were murmurs. I did not think he had convinced them at all but he had given them something to think about. I decided to add my own speech to Hurasu's, whether he wished it or not.

"Even the gods are with us on this, fearing what this evil man might do," I said, stretching the truth only a little. "The Ladies Yuza and Beyana have spoken to us."

There were many whispers now. I heard the name Beyana more than once. Zup spoke. "I have seen the Lady Beyana hunting across the mountains," said the old shaman, through Vuk. "Long ago. Long ago."

"We will have to think on this," broke in Mug. "What are your plans now, Yuzi?" I was both flattered and disturbed that he spoke to me as the leader here.

"We may scout south and see what this invader is up to," I told him.

Mug considered a moment. "I shall come with you. In the morning. Now, we must talk." With that, all the trolls went off together to debate in their own language. Hurasu might or might not have known something of that language but he did not attempt to eavesdrop.

"I am not sure you should have mentioned the goddesses," he said, but he did not sound overly concerned.

"You do not like gods," I said, as we walked toward the wide mouth of the cavern. Yeli and Sergi waited there.

"Not much," he admitted. "Some are not so bad. I am not sure about our sisters of the steppes."

"Turkic goddesses, originally? Are they the same as ones who were worshiped in my world?"

"Variants. There are infinite variants of everything and everyone, at least in potential. This Beyana and this Yuza are the goddesses these people know at this time. Perhaps a slightly different Beyana and Yuza will be known later and no one will realize it has changed. Not even the goddesses themselves."

That was more than I wanted to think about. "We may not know it but we know about it," came the voice of Beyana. We turned to see only the one goddess, emerging from the gloom along a rocky wall. Our friends, both those ahead and behind, were not looking this way. "We are who we are at this moment and this is enough." She held out her arms, looked herself up and down. "I am here and I am real."

"So you are," admitted Hurasu. "As you always were and always will be — in all your countless incarnations."

She laughed. "As long as time lasts. Maybe even after that!" She looked to me. "It was right to mention our names. It might be what those trolls need, though they are not, strictly speaking, worshipers. They know us."

"They know *you*," Hurasu pointed out.

"Quite so, oh mighty mortal! I hunt in their mountains at times, I and my hounds." She reached down to fondle the ear of one shaggy canine. "I think I shall send dreams tonight to help convince some of them. They shall believe them to be dreams, anyway. What simple troll could think that the Lady Beyana actually visited him?"

"Indeed, my lady," replied Hurasu. "It seems quite unlikely."

53. Scouting

It was not to be expected that the trolls actually made any decisions. However, some seemed quite agitated about something the next morning. Maybe their 'dreams' had done some good for our cause.

Mug was ready to go. Not Leni. "I'll go as far as the herds with you and no further," he said. "Let others seek adventures!"

"It would have been exhausting for Beyana last night," Hurasu confided to me as we set forth. "Even for gods, it is hard work crossing from world to world and repeatedly manifesting oneself." He walked on without saying more for a few seconds. "Or so I have been told. Gods do not let mortals in on their secrets very often."

"But you have had a long time to learn them."

"That is so." His eyes went to the south. "I doubt this Xahun has even half my years."

I had to laugh at that. "A youngster!"

He answered soberly, "That may be my greatest advantage."

Down out of the hills we walked. It would be a long journey to the reindeer herds; they were near their southernmost range now and would be working their way back north over the coming months. It was the second night when Hurasu decided to open to us, to let us understand — to the degree we were able — what drove him forward against Xahun.

It mattered little what he told me and the other men, though he seemed to address me. Much of it, too, I had heard already but not all put together. Maybe the troll Mug, across the fire from him, would take something from his words and carry it to his people.

"I have told you," he began, "I was concerned about the technological advances of your world, Yuzi. I was even more concerned when I realized a way had been found to force the gate open. It would take great power to do this, almost inconceivable power. The inventive people of your world are finding new ways to create such power. That does not matter now. Probably only Xahun knew how and I have warded the way."

"So you do not have to face him. You do not have to remain." I was willing to play along, whatever Hurasu's game might be.

"I could retreat. It might be wiser. The trolls are right when they say my enemy would probably ignore you and pass north. I could gather my strength in my stronghold and meet him later." He shook his head. There was a bitterness to his laugh. It seemed a little theatrical to me. "Ah, but he will grow stronger, and quickly. I fear if I am to defeat him it must be now."

"And if you battled him later, it might lay this world to waste. Is this not true?" It was what I had gleaned from things he had said, things the goddesses had said.

"It is. Whoever won might rule over desolation."

There was the point to it all. How much truth there was, I could not judge. I admit, I was more inclined at that point to be convinced by the words of the goddesses than those of Hurasu. This wizard might just want to dispose of a competitor. But again, Xahun had shown himself to be one who did evil, and Hurasu had not. I must remember that, and the threat he posed to Vasa.

When we reached the reindeer herders, there were reports of the army moving north. It was near, staying close to the coast. There had been loud noises, said one man, who had been grazing the reindeer in that area. It scared the herd and they had moved it north and west. That land bordered those of the wild trolls anyway, he said. It wasn't good to linger there overlong.

Gunfire? Maybe there had been a skirmish with the trolls. If they were hugging the seashore, the decision might have been to avoid them after that. These were only things I thought. Maybe the dragons had been keeping an eye on things and could tell us more. We hadn't seen one in a few days.

"We are almost as far south as the bay where you camped so long," said Mug. "Where I first saw you and wondered how so many men suddenly appeared."

It would be a good place to camp an army too, I thought. A pretty small army. Xahun had not that many more men than I had brought north. According to Sergi, not much over an hundred. The plan had been to bring through far more. "Maybe we should head there," I suggested. An hundred rifle-armed soldiers would be a formidable force in this land. We should go see.

And see only. There would be point in engaging. We were five men armed with spears. Oh, I did carry Sergi's sidearm, an old Nagant, not one of the newer Tokarevs. Seven shots the revolver held and was notoriously slow to reload. That did not matter for those seven cartridges were all we had. There had been a box of them in the airplane. Now those were at the bottom of the sea.

Halfway to the sea, a dragon slipped down to alight at a short distance. I could see it was not Sahra. Larger. Male? I was not sure how one told the difference. Nothing showed. Hurasu conferred and reported that our soldiers were where we had guessed. "We might as well go and get a look," I said. I didn't know what we could learn. Nothing of value, maybe, but Sergi might be able to offer some insights.

Hurasu was not so sure. Knowing their position might be enough. I think he was not fond of the idea of getting too close to Xahun. Not when he was on his own, and vulnerable. "He is unlikely to sense me but one can not be certain of all things."

"Never," agreed Mug.

"Then keep your distance," I told him, maybe a little more brusquely than I should. The idea of coming so far and doing nothing rankled. "Sergi and I will slip closer and get a better look." Mug might have come too, had I asked, but I wanted him to keep an eye on the other two. The former starshina did not object to me drafting him for this duty.

The others accompanied us some way before Hurasu simply said, "No further. We shall wait." We were still not within sight of the camp. It was perhaps another three kilometers before we spied it along the bay. They had chosen exactly the spot I had.

Hurasu had actually come fairly close, closer than he would have preferred, I am sure. We would make a quick scout, return to him, and be one our way north again. A high point I needed, where I could train my monocular on the soldiers and perhaps see some indication of Xahun's intentions. "Over there." The spot was only a little closer but should provide a decent vantage.

Sergi gazed toward the distant camp. "Those are my people," he breathed. "My regiment."

I turned to look more closely at him, saw his expression. Ah, I could understand the conflict in the starshina. "If you want to go back to them, I won't stop you." Better that than have him possibly betray me.

His eyes lingered on his former comrades for a few seconds longer be-fore he lowered them and shook his head. "No. I can not return, knowing what I know. Let's go."

We moved toward the point I had chosen, keeping ourselves low. It would be an excellent lookout position — and, of course, our opponent had thought of that too. The soldiers stationed there spied us; we had not been that cautious. Orders to halt rang out. Men with guns hurried our way and I heard calls from behind us. We were in the open. There was no place to hide.

54. Prisoners

"Give me the revolver, quickly," Sergi breathed. "They will think you are my prisoner."

I was not certain it was a good plan. But any other that came into my mind was worse. I immediately handed it over, belt and all. That would be more convincing. He strapped it around himself and trained the revolver on me. It was unlikely the soldiers could make any of this out clearly.

"I have him!" he called out. We were surrounded a minute or so later.

"Starshina Mikhailov?" asked one of the soldiers, recognizing the man despite his beard. He wore yet the remnants of his uniform. That would have helped.

"Take me to the captain," Sergi ordered. That was the way to do it. Don't waste your time explaining things to ordinary army men. A pair of them marched us into camp. Sergi kept the Nagant trained on me. It was not really necessary any longer!

A lieutenant came, not the captain. Not Xahun. Sergi gave him a pretty good story of taking me prisoner and escaping. "Maybe," concluded the starshina, "he will want to come back to his brothers in the Red Army. He is a good Russian boy." It was a nice added touch.

We were left standing for some time — typical of the army — while this officer went to speak to his commander. "Captain Zahunsky wants to see you," he reported on his return. "The prisoner only."

Sergi was already regaling the soldiers with largely fictitious tales of his captivity as I was led off. Xahun had his headquarters out on the same point I had chosen. His large tent did look somewhat more comfortable than my seal skin cover. The tank was positioned here, its gun trained on the approach from land. A commodious two-wheeled cart sat near it.

Xahun was standing by a folding table, looking toward the sea. When he turned to me I could see he was holding a sextant. "Fifty-five degrees south latitude, more or less," he said. "It will as cold as Mother Russia in the winter!" The mustache he had worn had given way to a full beard. No need to maintain a military appearance here.

The man looked me over. "Where is Sossinsky?" he growled at an aide. "Bring him here!"

Moments later, a small man entered, leaning on a crutch. I looked down, saw the empty trouser leg. "Lieutenant," I greeted him.

He stared at me a moment before recognition came. "No longer," he muttered.

Xahun nodded in satisfaction. "One of your people then."

"Dobrov," came the answer. "Komandir Dobrov." The lieutenant looked at me more steadily now. "How?"

"How indeed?" asked Xahun. He looked over some papers he pulled from a leather folder. "Ah, Josef Dobrov." The man nodded and turned his attention back to me. "You were one of those who disappeared after the train wreck. Sossinsky was the lone survivor from the troop car, and only because he had stepped outside and was thrown clear before it went over the precipice. I had him attached to my command. I knew, of course, what had become of you and the others who vanished." His eyes flickered to Sossinsky. "Go," he ordered. The lieutenant hobbled away.

"I also have seen you in another's mind." He smiled at my reaction to this. "So you understand these things. This is good. Have a seat, Komandir." He waved me toward a camp stool.

"It is long since I have worn that rank," I said, sitting. "It means nothing here."

"True. These men will realize that eventually." He waved an arm toward the camp, before taking another stool. "A man who understands this world and what is going on would be useful."

I made no comment so he went on. "You understand some about the gate, do you not? That it takes massive amounts of energy to open it. I thought at first it was the wind but it is more the lightning and an interaction between the two forces. A charged vortex. An electrical cyclone! That is as good and as imprecise a description as any. I was able to pry it open just a little with a battery of generators, and peek through. Maybe if nuclear power were ever achieved it could be blown open permanently.

"Ah you like that not! Me neither, to be honest. It does not matter now, my boy. I finally generated enough power to come here and it is just as well that door is shut behind me. I never liked that idea of the Soviet army invading anyway. It was only a selling point, so they would back my research. But I did want an army to come through, an army I command-ed. That is why I did not sit patiently and wait, once I knew the proper location. It might have been years or decades, but eventually it would have opened."

It was quite a speech. "So what now, Lord Xahun?"

He was momentarily surprised by my use of the name. "Perhaps you know *too* much, Dobrov." He studied me for a moment. "You must be closer to this Hurasu than I had realized."

"I know him." I attempted to sound nonchalant.

"Hmm. Well enough he might attempt a rescue? No, he is not that stupid. He knows how well I will ward myself and this place. And no men of this world could face my soldiers." He motioned to a guard. "Keep this man under arrest, guarded at all times. The one who brought him in too. I do not trust him."

I was not surprised Sergi no longer had his weapon when we were re-united. They put us on the beach, where the only escape was up the ravine that ran between the cliffs. The man took his misfortune cheer-fully enough. "It was a gamble," he said, shrugging.

"I am not sure you are disbelieved," I told him. "Xahun is cautious. And I think he hopes to use me, perhaps turn me to his cause."

"Not to be trusted," was Sergi's opinion. It was one with which I agreed. The next day, the starshina was taken away to be questioned. He never returned.

55. On the March

"Traitors are executed. Once we learn what is to be learned."

Had I not already chosen to oppose this evil man, I would have then. I did not care whether he was a danger to this world. I did not care that he had left another world broken in his wake. He had coldly, brutally slain a man who had proven himself a loyal friend. Not to mention all he had done to Vasa.

"And we did learn things," he continued. "So your wizard hides in the north? I will destroy him if he sets himself against me." Xahun laughed a mad laugh, a mocking laugh. "I will destroy him anyway!"

I could only thank Sergi for not revealing that Hurasu had been nearby. Even under torture, he had remained loyal.

And this Xahun. I had thought him but a ruthless, ambitious man, the sort I had met more than once before. He was something far worse. He was an empty creature that would never be able to fill itself, a ravening nihilist hoping to swallow all existence. Ah, you knew I was a poet. Allow me this. I know no better way to put it.

Perhaps there was a Xahun inside of Hurasu, one he kept under control. If so, I admired the sorcerer. But I could be of no help to him here.

Xahun continued speaking as if it were but normal conversation. "I hate to leave my tank but fuel has run low. The cart it pulled too; we shall have to divide all our supplies among the men. We all march today, Josef, even the captain." He was leaving no one here. His little army would carry what it needed for a swift march and the rest would sit here, perhaps never to be reclaimed. A world lay ahead, and all its wealth.

"Walk beside me," he ordered. "There is much you could tell me, I think, but I have not the time to take it from you. And —" His voice became intimate, solicitous. "I think you might serve me of your own will. There is much I can give you, Josef. Including Vasa."

He smiled knowingly at my reaction. "Or I could take her away. It is your choice."

We did not march too rapidly. Sossinsky was able to keep up, at least this day. Xahun wearied of my taciturnity after a time and sent me further back in the column. No one prevented me from walking with my former commander.

"I thought Zahunsky was a madman until he actually opened that damnable door," said Sossinsky. "Now I know he is."

"How did he convince anyone to back him?" The whole idea of a gate to another world seemed preposterous on the face of it, a crackpot's dream.

"Your disappearance had much to do with it. He had been pushing his theories for years without much official interest. Then he held you up as proof." He turned to look at me. "Did all on your car escape death?"

"We did. In the Urals, that is. Some have been killed here. Very few." We had been lucky. "Ivan Andreyev is still with me. We lost Orlov."

I am not sure he even remembered the two soldiers. "I do not know where this Zahunsky came from," Sossinsky said, "or how he formed his theories. Little was told to me. He just wanted me along in case — well, in case he came on one like you."

"Not theories," I answered, "and where he came from was yet another world. It was not the first time he has passed through a gate."

Sossinsky had no ready reply to that. But a minute later, he asked, "So the captain is not Russian at all?"

"No. His name is Xahun." I was not going to say anything about Atlantis. That might be too much. "His people are, um, quite long lived." I was not going to mention thousands of years, either.

"And now he hopes to conquer this world. For himself, not the Soviet Union."

"That is so." I hesitated before adding, "And I oppose him, I and my friends. I and my adopted people."

"Perhaps I should too," said Sossinsky, "but I am not sure how."

"All one can do is wait for an opportunity," I replied.

It is not to be thought that I spoke with no one else. The soldiers were interested in me and in this world and I told my tale more than once. I emphasized that this was a new world but did not go so far as to as say they no longer need serve Xahun. He would not have countenanced that. But that thought hid behind my words. The men could not help but see things had changed.

The next day, those men began to get sick. I recognized it as what we had called the Troll Fever — not life threatening but it would slow this march. Sergi or I or both had carried it to them, undoubtedly. I was glad my friend could get one last lick in. It hit Sossinsky hard; I helped him keep up as best I could. He would probably have been left behind otherwise.

Was that such a bad idea? If any of my friends followed, they could pick him up. Or wild trolls could eat him. It would be a chance. Would that I could communicate some way, any way!

Not with the dragons. I saw them, high up, a couple times. The soldiers did not recognize them for what they were. How could they? If they noticed them at all, they would have thought them birds. I did not know about Xahun. Even if he knew of dragons, he would have no reason to think they spied on him.

As I lay awake at night, listening to the wretched former lieutenant coughing, I wondered if it would be so difficult for me myself to escape. These were soldiers, yes, and they had guns and pretty good discipline. The fear of their captain saw to that! But I had been living a life that had both hardened the body and sharpened the mind. I would take my chance against any one of them. Except Xahun. If he even came close to matching Hurasu physically, he would be a formidable fighter.

I looked at Sossinsky's crutch lying at his side, and the cap he always wore. I slipped the cap onto my head, pulling it low to shade my face, wrapped myself in my blanket, placed the crutch beneath my arm, and made myself as small as possible. The latrine was that way. I hobbled toward it, coughing a little now and then. So far did I make it with no challenge.

There would be sentries further out. If I slipped into the tall heather now, I might be able to crawl past them and away. It was a chance. If I was caught, Xahun would order me shot. This I did not doubt at all. I thought I might chance it anyway.

Then my thoughts went to Sossinsky. Would they think he aided me? Would they care? He might be made a scapegoat regardless. Even if not, I doubted he could keep up with tomorrow's march. Maybe not even with my help. I cursed and returned to the sleeping man.

Tomorrow might bring one of those opportunities I had spoken of. I lay down and slept soundly enough to dawn.

56. Deserters

Sossinsky seemed better in the morning. Tired, though. He might or might not be able to march all day. But a stronger Sossinsky would have a better chance of survival if left behind. I explained all this to him, whispering. He nodded as I told him there was no guarantee he would be found or rescued.

He already knew of the troll cannibals. The troops had encountered them. I told him there were 'good' trolls and, indeed, it was likely one or two followed us. Mug would be inclined to do that. The man thought maybe it was a good plan. He was very tired of walking, too. I told him to say 'Yuzi' to anyone who came on him, and gave him the word for 'friend,' and advised him the best direction to travel would be back to their camp on the bay, if he met no one. So rather than rise that morning, he remained wrapped in his blanket, moaning and seemingly delirious. The men wanted to carry him with us. Xahun ordered him left where he was. He did not disappoint there.

I watched that lone supine figure fade as we marched on. Good luck to you, Lieutenant! At least the soldiers had left him some rations and water. We were progressing slower than Xahun might have wished but we were progressing none the less. The track their leader chose was closer to the sea than the one I and my people had taken. He would not be crossing over the hills by our usual path if he kept to it. Still, he would pass close to our village and even closer to the one on the bay. I would expect him to occupy the latter.

My friends would know this. They would not let themselves be caught there. A retreat into the hills would be simple and Xahun would be too impatient to root them out. Unless he knew Hurasu was with them; then he might consider it worthwhile.

Still, he would march on in time, not wishing to be in the south through winter, nor even on Nagi perhaps. The folk in the north would not be able to get out of his way so easily, though their shamans would warn them. No need to worry about that right now. In fact, my only worry was how to get away from this army. Away from Xahun.

It was then the attacks began. Only at night. A thrown spear or a sentry picked off. I thought trolls likely. So did the soldiers. Friendly trolls or the wild ones? I suspected the former. When Xahun called for me, I assured him the latter. "There are many savage trolls in the interior, little more than animals." That was the truth.

He gave me a look of disdain. "Undoubtedly. Yet I have felt the minds of wise troll shamans. Some, I know, are your friends and allies."

There was no point in denying it. There was no point in admitting it either, so I said nothing. "Why do you help them?" he asked. "These are not your people."

"They have become my people. For now, anyway. My duty is to them, to those who have adopted me, to those I led here."

"Oh, I see who you are now, Josef," he said. "You will never serve me. It is unfortunate." He looked me up and down. "You are like *him*."

I knew he meant Hurasu. Maybe I was. I decided it was a compliment. "Still," he continued, "it would be foolish to throw you away. You may yet serve in some bargain." He turned from me as he marched on, seemingly as indefatigable as his enemy Hurasu. I recognized this as a dismissal and dropped back.

It was the next day the traitors came. I recognized them, a handful of the men I had led into this land. Eight they were. A couple I knew for career criminals, the rest ordinary men who has run afoul of the law. What had led them to make this choice? These were some of the men I had spoken to, the ones who seemed dissatisfied, who had been eager to hear of Xahun. I was happy, though, that Anna was not with them, nor Tani.

Traitors? Perhaps that is harsh. They owed me nothing. If they did not like it here, they were free to move on. That I might do myself. But if they aided this invader against the people who had taken them in, I would not hesitate to kill any one of them myself.

Xahun welcomed them, treated them well. That was to be expected. Their knowledge, though not extensive, was valuable, and they could speak the language. Shortly, they were marching along with us. "Ho, Hetman," said one. "I see you too have joined this captain."

"I march with him," I allowed. Let him make what he would of it. I am sure they all figured out my status quickly enough.

Three I saw slip away later. I was surprised this was allowed. What if they were spies rather than true recruits? "They promised to bring back some reindeer," one of the starshinas told me. "We could use some fresh meat." So now they were going to steal from those who had fed them. They would know something of reindeer and could probably cut two or three from the herd quietly. A troop this size needed more than that.

They did not return. My guess was that they had been caught at their thievery. Perhaps by trolls, in which case they would be dead. The men of this land would have simply sent them back, most likely. Maybe even with reindeer. Or maybe they did desert back to the other side. There was no way of knowing then. Xahun let no more men leave.

The soldiers themselves were growing restless. I could hear it, could feel it. "Why are we marching north?" one asked. "Won't it be colder there?" Many did not understand they were in the southern hemisphere. Most did not grasp that it was another world. But slowly this would become evident. Then would they still follow Xahun? Only if he threw them into battle, made them invaders so they had no choice but to fight to survive. No choice but to follow him. Xahun would not want peace.

What good was it for me to march on with them? I had chosen not to attempt an escape once. There was no reason to do so again. Before Xahun decided to kill me, when he decided I could be of no use. Would that I could get close enough to attack him myself! No chance of that. Too many soldiers around him, soldiers still loyal, and he was far too cautious. Moreover, I had no doubt he could best me in any fight.

Yes, escape. I must watch for the opportunity.

57. Escapes

The opportunity came that night. No one guarded me that closely, but there was always a double perimeter of sentries. Also, I stood out, being the only one in leather among all those uniforms. That had changed a little with the new arrivals in their native clothing.

I heard commotion off to the southeast. Another attack in the night? A little later, a wounded man was borne in, carried bodily as litters were considered unnecessary baggage on this march. "Not badly wounded," said one of the soldiers with them. "A spear in the shoulder. We've patched him up so he can march in the morning." He had carried the hurt man's gun and overcoat back, and laid these down beside the soldier. An hour later, the camp had died down and the wounded soldier slept. I had sat beside him as the soldiers, one by one, decided they were unneeded and went off to find their own bedrolls or to report for sentry duty.

It would be a repeat of my previous aborted attempt. I slipped on the overcoat and the man's helmet, slowly rose, sliding the sling of his rifle over my shoulder. There was always a latrine trench. Digging it was the first order of a new camp. I headed that direction. A man passed on his way back, and nodded amiably in the darkness.

I hunkered down, as if using the trench and, seeing no eyes looking my direction, rolled onto the ground. So far. So far. No noise. No one had noticed. I slowly crept forward on elbows and into the heather. That was a start. Now to get past the sentries.

Ha, I probably could have walked right out to them dressed so, clubbed one and ran. It might have had as good a chance. I writhed forward, a veritable snake in the grass. Maybe Yuza could help a poor snake, eh? The sentries were — there, and there. Close enough together to keep an eye on each other. It would be hard to slip between. And wouldn't there be another ring outside them? Not very far outside them. Close enough they could be seen. Yes, there, ahead.

Forward a few more feet. I shed the overcoat. It impeded me. So did the rifle but I chose to keep it. It was overcast. Misty rain fell. This was very much to the good. It was also fairly typical at this time of year. I was glad the sentries stayed rooted to one spot. I might have had them moving, were I commanding here. Probably not Xahun's doing. I doubt he paid much attention, leaving it to the lieutenant and the starshinas.

Now I must get past these last men. They were more nervous. I did not blame them at all, standing at the outer edge of the camp, looking into darkness, knowing there were those out there who might strike at any moment. They probably knew they might be eaten, too. That sort of thing, though meaningless, truly, helps create terror in men.

Of a sudden, I found myself face to face with someone crawling the opposite direction. A troll. "Friend," I whispered. He had probably already figured that out. He seemed to be trying to make my face out in the dark.

"Yuzi," he said. "Come." He turned himself around and we both crawled outward. I don't think I knew his name but a number of trolls would have seen me at some time or another. There might be more of them concealed around us. No, Yuzi, there *were* more of them. That was a certainty. I heard the call of the night plover. My companion returned it, adding a different note. Back and forth the signals went and then a commotion arose further south. "A diversion," whispered the troll when we got out a little further, where the lights of the camp were no more than those of the stars. "You saved a man tonight. We would have taken that sentry."

There were other bodies around us now. I heard my name whispered, as if being passed down a line. "Back to camp," came an order. I recognized it as Mug's voice. In a couple minutes we were on our feet and the troll was walking beside me. "I was wondering how we would rescue you," he said.

"I became tired of waiting and decided to rescue myself," I responded.

"Maybe you would have made it," he mused. "Maybe you wouldn't. Your friend is with us. It is good you gave him words to use."

"Sossinsky? I am glad of this." I was not sure why, really. The lieutenant had never actually been a friend. I had owed nothing to him, yet I had made him another obligation. Another duty. Ah, it was the right thing to do, I told myself.

"We speak to him through Leni. Best you take him north now, though, and teach him your language." He seemed to be considering something before going on. "We would kill a crippled man in our tribe."

"It seems Xahun was willing to do the same. Be that as it may, Sossinsky has useful knowledge. I would not waste it." That might have been rationalization of my actions.

It was still dark when we reached the camp. It was a dark and cold camp, and both men and trolls were there. Mug rummaged in some skins and pulled out a revolver. "Andri had this when we found him. He held it in front of him while screaming 'Yuzi' and 'friend.'"

Andri? Andrey, that must be. I had never use Sossinsky's first name, though I knew it. "Might as well give it back to him," I decided. I had another rifle now. It was no better than the rifles we had before but there was ammunition!

Sossinsky accepted the Nagant in the morning. "I appropriated poor Mikhailov's sidearm when he was arrested. No one seemed to be paying any attention to it."

"Prudent," I commented.

"So I thought. I was so disoriented when your, um, friends found me I could not have hit anything."

The way home was slow. Home, yes. Where else would I call home? Sossinsky — Andri — was healthy enough but his limp slowed him. A long road it was, and Xahun's army might be progressing more quickly on their own path. Where was Hurasu while all this was going on? That he had remained I had little doubt. The sorcerer would not run away nor neglect an obligation. Xahun was right about him. Maybe he was even right about me.

There was time to give Andri language lessons on the way. Leni had remained behind; he had no desire to fight anyone but his knowledge of Russian might again come in handy. Into the hills. It would not be so long before the reindeer came over them again. Summer was winding down and all my plans to leave this place in the spring were only dreams I could no longer remember clearly.

At last we stood above the village, my village. Andri's village, if he wished. He looked down and pulled out his cigarette case. "The last one," he laughed. "I think this is the time to smoke it, before starting my new life."

He inhaled the last time, letting the blue smoke drift from his nostrils, as we entered the village, and cast the butt aside.

58. Catching Up

"I thought I might join them" Anna said. "I was tempted until we had word of what that monster did to poor Sergi. The trolls found his body when the army marched away, discarded on the beach." If Vuk were with them, word would have gotten back quickly. I didn't see him in their camp. "Some, that did not bother, but I have seen too much of such things and such men."

"And I spent too much time serving them," said Sossinsky.

"Did we have a choice?" I asked.

"We did. We could have been like Yeli here." He nodded toward the man. "We could have fought back, one way or another."

"And been on the way to the work camps with the rest of us," laughed Anna. We strode on toward Ati's house. These two had attached themselves to us as soon as we had appeared.

"So where is everyone else?" I asked.

"Vasa and Ashaga are with Ati, I think. Ashaga would be with Konosi, were he here, but he has gone off to the bay to help prepare for that — man's coming." I hoped none of them had any idea of fighting. "The two of them are married now. Olga performed the ceremony while you were gone." Anna looked up at me. "I think your capture made them decide time was short."

"Made Konosi think it was short, anyway," spoke Yeli. "So Telpata and I married at the same time." And Leni had said not a word about it.

Hurasu? No one had mentioned him. I would let Vasa fill me in.

"He remains in the hills, preparing for what will come," she told me. "The battle." Only she sat with Ati; Ashaga was off somewhere else, maybe to give us privacy. Nor had the others entered the shaman's house. "In the end, he knows it will be he against Xahun."

"We all knew this, I think," spoke Ati.

"So he will come when he wishes," I said. "When he is ready." I thought on that. "Or maybe when Xahun is ready.'

Vasa nodded. "I think that is it. He hopes to wear him down some first, to frustrate him. He is in no hurry but this invader is."

"And we are caught between." It sounded cynical but was also true. "As long as Xahun can be made to play his game. He might just decide to march on north."

"Anything is possible," admitted the old shaman. "Why don't you two run along? I'll let Hurasu know you arrived."

We did run along, and pretty quickly. I had much missed my Vasa — and maybe all she represented. We slipped into the house Ashaga and Konosi shared; with her new husband gone — a quite incomprehensible act on the priest's part, in my opinion — she was staying with Ati.

It was good to hold Vasa, to love her. To be with her. Why would I ever want to be anywhere else? I couldn't think of a reason right then.

A voice. "I do hope I am not interrupting anything important."

Fortunately, not at the moment. "Lady Yuza," I greeted her, rolling over to get a look at the tall goddess. Vasa peeked at her over the edge of the bear skin. There was no sign of her sister this time.

She guessed my thoughts. "Beyana is probably with Hurasu again. He and my sister have been spending much time together."

And I thought he avoided gods. "Let us hope something good comes of it," I said.

I thought Yuza would not stop laughing. "Maybe a niece or nephew," she said. "I have not seen Beyana smitten in millennia." She settled down to a more thoughtful expression. "That, of course, is up to my sister. We can choose to conceive, or not. It is good that you are home safely, Yuzi."

Vasa managed to get some words out, in a very small voice. "Couldn't you have helped him, my lady?" This girl who had spoken to gods from afar was not so confident when one came into her bedchamber.

The goddess shook her head emphatically. "Xahun and his camp were far too well warded. We could only have entered by becoming completely mortal."

"And then you would have no powers." Vasa nodded in understanding.

"So it is, little one." She peered at the girl. "This one *is* powerful. Hurasu is right about her."

"Could she and, um, Hurasu, and maybe even you sort of gang up on this Xahun. Three or four against one?"

Vasa giggled. "It doesn't work that way. A spell is a spell is a spell."

A broad smile from Yuza. "An old truism among wizards. Not technically accurate, maybe, but correct none the less. Two wizards combined are no more powerful than one."

"Although dealing with multiple opponents might wear one down more quickly," added Vasa. "That's what Hurasu said. Ati doesn't know anything about attacking with magic." I could see her brow furrow between the lengths of straight brown hair that fell on either side. "And that's good."

"So it's more like a sword fight," I said.

"Exactly," agreed the goddess. "We will continue to test that sorcerer, if only to remind him we are here. I and my sister and Hurasu and maybe even some of the shamans. Maybe you, little girl. But we will not engage him. Not yet."

"We'll hammer on his door and run away," giggled Vasa.

"It will have to be us. None of my family feel the need to help. Some pay no attention to the mortal worlds anyway."

This made Vasa think of something. She seemed completely at ease with this tall and terrible and beautiful goddess now. "Benesi isn't from your family, is he?"

"Different pantheon, but we get along well enough. The people around here don't know my family very much, not like in the north."

"I should try to talk to him again," Vasa decided.

"Be careful of him. He's as randy as I am," warned Yuza, and then turned an appraising eye on us. "Hmm, you two — no, of course not. You'll see me later," she promised, and summoned that writhing smoke around her, disappearing into its depths.

"I can't figure that out," I said. "Does she turn into smoke?"

"What? Oh, no, she is just pulling smoke from somewhere to hide her disappearing act."

"Oh." That was somehow disappointing.

"She is stepping back into her own world," Vasa added.

"Can you see that world. Um, visit it?"

"Maybe. But better to give the gods their privacy, isn't it?"

"They haven't given us much. Now — where were we?"

59. A Raid

Konosi returned to us the next day, along with many who fled from the village by the bay. Chances were Xahun's forces were occupying it by the time they arrived here. That meant the enemy was only a day away if they chose to turn this direction. We would know. Scouts were watching. The dragons were watching.

"They could find far worse places to hole up for the winter, if they decided to stay," claimed Mazi. "But we dismantled the boats. They aren't going to be using those." There were plenty of houses, maybe enough for that whole contingent of the Red Army. But they didn't have enough supplies and didn't know the country. They would starve.

We had to be ready to run at a minute's warning. Food supplies had already been shifted elsewhere. These people had not dawdled while I was gone. It will be said that some felt they should share those supplies. They did not see the difference between this invading army and the refugees I had brought them a year earlier.

Maybe there was none, not in the men themselves. It was Xahun who made that difference.

By evening of that day, Hurasu had also returned. Quietly, alone, with no notice, he walked into the village and sat beside the fire ring at its center, the place where the elders would meet. Many of us gathered to hear what he would say.

"The only way this can be ended is with me facing my foe. We must find a way to force him away from the protection of his army."

"And you can defeat him then?" asked Olga.

"I do not know," admitted the sorcerer. "If I fall, he will march on, this I know. You will be safe." He paused. "For a time."

"These empty lands might never be much affected by his ambitions," I said. This I had thought on, this I had concluded. There was little here to interest Xahun.

"This may be so."

"He still wants me," said Vasa.

"But not enough to spend time in pursuit," I told her. "There are other things he wants more." I believed this to be so.

"So we should continue to harass those soldiers," spoke Konosi.

"Starve them," said someone further back. "They'll desert soon enough."

"That would take time," spoke another voice.

"Yes," agreed Hurasu. "Too much time. Xahun would move on without facing me." He sighed. "Were his wardings not so strong, dreams might be sent to those men. Dreams of doubt and fear." Most did not understand this, but I saw Ati nod knowingly.

Maybe the annoyances of which Vasa and Yuza had spoken could break the evil sorcerer's attention and let some of that protection slip. I did not know of such things. And that too, might take too long.

"They would starve right now," came a woman's voice, "if someone could destroy their food stores." It was Anna. Good advice, too, but difficult to achieve.

"Then let us do it," said Konosi. "Let us do more than just harass." There were murmurs of agreement all around, perhaps more from those I had led here than those born to this village. Many of those, I think, still preferred to hide, for the most part, and let this crisis pass.

"A raid," said Hurasu. "I fear I can not accompany you, though I would greatly desire it. Xahun might sense me." His eyes went to me. "Yuzi should lead you."

I hated to admit it but he was right. I would know more of those soldiers and their camp than anyone. "We'll need the trolls to help," I said. They had surely kept close to the army. "And the dragons," I added. "You will have to translate for us." This I directed to Hurasu.

"Of course," he replied. "They can at least tell us where the stores are kept." I had other thoughts on what they might do but kept those to myself.

By the next morning we were on our way. Halfway there — more or less — Sahra spiraled down to us. I was fairly sure it was she. "She tells me they have not put their supplies inside the houses," Hurasu said. "That's a good thing," That was his opinion, not Sahra's.

"They want to be able to march immediately, maybe," I said. It was not a great amount of material anyway, neither food nor military supplies.

The men had needed to carry it all in packs on their march, and anything not absolutely needed had been left in the south. It was not entrusted to those individual soldiers when they made camp, but placed in a central cache. "There will be no expectation of an attack from the direction of the sea. We can engage all their attention if we show ourselves on this side."

I explained my plan and he relayed it to the dragon. "It will mean exposing yourselves," he said to me. "You will have casualties." I nodded. I was aware of the dangers. Then a smile. "But Sahra has a much better idea than having the dragons attempt to steal the supplies. Quicker and easier too."

What that was, I did not know but if they both thought it a good plan, then so did I. "I will come no closer to Xahun," said Hurasu as Sahra flew away, "but I shall remain at this spot, if able."

It was foolhardy, of course, to attack the soldiers ahead. The weapons of my people were not suited to long range use, though both Ivan and I had loaded rifles. We could do damage with those. We would not attempt to conserve our ammunition. And we would certainly attack under cover of darkness. Partial darkness at this time of year. The trolls joined us as we marched nearer, around the middle of the afternoon. Some forty we were, all together. More were not necessary.

There was still plenty of light when we drew near enough to spy our enemy. The bulk of them would be down on the slope, some maybe in the houses though the weather was good enough. Ha, good enough for me, one who had become accustomed to it. They might think it quite miserable. Sentries patrolled above. We two with the rifles should pick high points where we could use our weapons to best advantage. "You over there, Vani," I said. So had Ivan come to be named here. I picked a spot on the other side of our force. We waited for more darkness. Where was Xahun down there? Would that I could get him in my sights!

Most unlikely. I could see, from here, men and trolls creeping forward. Only because I knew where to look. Here there were no sentries on a high place; they would need have been too far from the main force, too vulnerable. That was to the good. If one of the attackers was spied, that would be the signal to charge. Otherwise, I left it to Mug, near the center, to decide.

He cried out some sort of troll war-cry and it was on. Our men had moved close enough to overwhelm the outer line of sentries without problem nor even a shot being fired in defense. Now came the battle. The second line was not so open, so vulnerable, and the call had come out to those troops below. Best we keep them from coming up and into the open as much as possible. Their rifles would be impossible to withstand then. I yet held my fire. When it is needed, Yuzi, when it is needed.

There, the Red soldiers were breaking through the spears that had kept them back and unable to fire effectively. I trained the Mosin Nagant on one and fired. Vani's rifle sounded a few seconds later. Don't hurry, boy, pick your targets. Me too, I told myself. Our job now was more to cover the retreat of our raiders than anything else as they faded back into the half-light of nearly night, to hide themselves among the rolling hills. They had drawn out the soldiers. That was the task.

I looked beyond those soldiers. Three dragons skimmed along the surface of the bay and up the slope, swiftly and with none there to stop them. Most of the defenders never knew they were there. They alit beside a small, tarp-covered mound, all quickly turning away from it, planting their feet, and raising their tails.

A hideous stench wafted toward us on the sea breeze.

60. Hunger

"They used their fire on the supply cache," explained Hurasu. "You knew dragons had fire, did you not?" The question was put to me with a straight face.

"But they were not, um, breathing it." That I was able to see.

"No, it comes from the other end. The dragon is related to the weasel family and has the same ability to spray a noxious liquid. More than noxious with a dragon." The sorcerer grinned broadly. "Yon soldiers will not be able to eat any of what was stored."

"I hope it was worth it," I said. Four men and trolls we had left dead, others had made it back wounded. But we had certainly slain at least twice that number ourselves. Neither Vani nor I had any more cartridges. I would carry a rifle no longer.

Unless, of course, we liberated some more ammunition. That should still be usable even after an encounter with dragon fire. I knew the food that was ruined was not all that much. The soldiers would have run out soon, anyway, instead of right now. What would they do? Or what would Xahun do? They would still follow him, at least for a time.

On the second day, we learned they were marching toward us. We were prepared, had been prepared. Most of the villagers left. All of the food did. They would find nothing here. "The men who deserted would have some idea of hiding places," I told the others.

"Not of great importance," felt Hurasu. "They would not bother attempting to root them out. But they will know of your herds and that they are moving north. All the meat they might want if they go and get it."

"So when they find this place stripped they should head across the hills," I said.

Mug smiled. "A good place for ambushes." Accordingly, we fighters also retreated into the hills, leaving the village empty. There was no guarantee Xahun would act as we anticipated. He would not want to, would know the risks. But his men would surely not follow him anywhere else. I guessed there were maybe eighty of those left, and all armed with rifles. They would not be easily dealt with.

Three days those soldiers crawled into the hills. From time to time a spear came from the dark, a sentry disappeared. We called out in the night, telling them they would be fed if they left Zahunsky. It was for me and Vani to do this at first; later Sossinsky joined us and helped in it. Men knew his voice. Whether that mattered any, I am not sure, but there were deserters, more each night. That included most of those who had deserted us! No point in thinking to punish them. They no longer mattered in this conflict.

Xahun must have sensed his foe's closeness now, for Hurasu made no attempt to maintain a distance. He might even be speaking to him. I was not let in on this, nor was Vuk, the only shaman there, certain. "He might be taunting his enemy," the troll hazarded. "He might be challenging him. They must fight eventually." So had Hurasu told me, and he had not be certain of his own victory.

On the fourth day, Hurasu called out, "Face me, Xahun, and let us finish this!" He did this in Russian, having me give him the proper words, so the soldiers would understand. Each few minutes as the enemy moved further he repeated the challenge. Needless to say, we also continued to call out for the soldiers to desert, telling them the quarrel was only with their leader. The column ground to a halt shortly after midday. Xahun cried out in a language none understood.

"The tongue of Atlantis," whispered Hurasu. "Never did I expect to hear it again." He called a response and the two shouted back and forth for a while. "It is done," he said at last. "We will meet in the morning and test each other. We may bring a few men but no rifles on either side." Xahun did not know our rifles were useless.

"A physical battle?" asked Konosi.

"Both physical and magical," was the reply. "Much will happen you can not see nor understand. Now I need to sleep." With that, the sorcerer went off a short way, lay down, and fell asleep at once.

I thought I might as well do the same but my attempt to slumber was once again interrupted. Both goddesses came, and Beyana looked more than upset. "He is foolish to go against this man," she maintained. "We both know Xahun is the more powerful."

"But your Hurasu is cunning," said her sister. "Far more experienced."

"And there is naught we can do?" I asked.

"You could shoot him with your strange weapon," came Beyana's immediate response.

"Those no longer work. And they were forbidden from the meeting." I studied the goddess a moment. "What of your own bow? Might you get a shot while the two are busy with each other?"

"It is possible, but I doubt it. I know how they will set up their fight, with both warding and men ringing them in."

"Then all we can do is trust in Hurasu. And if he fails — then we must find some other plan."

"There will be no other plan," spoke Yuza, quite emphatically. "Xahun will have won, and my sister and I shall go home."

Leaving us to our own devices. So it would be.

61. The Duel

"There is something I must tell you," spoke Hurasu, as he prepared for his meeting with Xahun. "It is of Vasa."

I nodded. I waited. "Has she ever said anything of her family? No? Very well. I asked her of her father." He paused. "The girl did not want to speak of him, but she admitted she did not know who he was. Her mother was raped during the war. A soldier or a brigand; exactly which does not matter."

"Does this matter?" I asked. Where the man going?

"I have said before Vasa might be one of my own descendants. But her father — I believe he was Xahun. It explains her power." He looked steadily into my face. "I did not and shall not tell her this."

"Neither shall I," I replied. It truly did not matter.

"However, I must warn you," continued Hurasu, and now the slightest of smiles came to his hawk-like visage. "Your Vasa may prove very long lived. Let us be on our way."

That was certainly something to think about! We met our opponent and his party in a small bowl of a valley, near at hand.

"Ah, Sossinsky! So you survived. I am impressed." Xahun surveyed the group that had accompanied Hurasu, six of us. He looked to the eight he had brought. "You two," he ordered. "Leave.

"We will make this all according to the rules," the sorcerer said, turning back to Hurasu. "Form a ring," he called out.

"Not too close," added Hurasu, in our own tongue, "and alternate by which side you belong to." He held his silver sword carelessly, his eyes on Xahun, his face expressionless. We did as we were told. Xahun drew a long saber from its scabbard, an ordinary-enough Russian army sword.

"I have no steel of Atlantis," he laughed. "But this can kill you every bit as effectively." Then we understood no more, for both switched to the tongue of their birth. There seemed to be a — dome around and over them. Not easy to see in the light of day for it seemed, too, to be made of light. Colors shifted in it, golds and blues and a sickly green that seemed to emanate from Xahun. The men's mouths moved but I could hear no words. Their swords met.

No advantage to either and they moved back. There was an unseen battle going on, more important, maybe, than the one with swords. Yet I suspected that one of those swords would end this struggle. Did a part of each, a part they had sent elsewhere, battle in other worlds? Could they draw on those other worlds, as I had seen Hurasu do before, to aid them?

The last question was answered swiftly, for lightning flashed and crashed, almost certainly directed by Hurasu toward his enemy. Xahun stopped it with a gesture and perhaps a slight smile. Again they came at each other with their swords, battling longer this time. Both were far more skilled than any fencer I had ever seen. Both were faster and more agile than any man I had ever seen. I would last no more than seconds against either.

An inadvertent shiver. If Xahun won, none could oppose his will. He could slay me on a whim or make me his slave. The two disengaged again, lowering their swords and glaring at each other. Evenly matched, I thought. A mistake by either could give the other the advantage. Or stamina might ultimately play a role, though I strongly suspected both were capable of going on like this for hours, maybe even days.

Now Xahun brought an attack from some other world. A rain of some sort. Hurasu shielded himself from it but it sizzled where it hit the ground. That sort of thing was seemingly ineffective, perhaps intended only to feel out their opponents. They would have to fight more directly.

Which they did, sword clashing on sword. That they continued to battle elsewhere too, I did not doubt. One thing I noted — Xahun was cautious about using his blade against Hurasu's. I suspected it was of a weaker metal, that if the two swords truly were tested one against the other, the blade from my own world would be the one to fail.

It would never be learned which was truly the better, for that is when Xahun cheated. Yes, despite his protestations of following the rules. His men carried no rifles but I saw one surreptitiously sliding a handgun, an automatic, from his pocket. I cried out, I leaped in his direction, but not before one shot rang out. Then I had him down, the gun in the dirt. The others ringed us about, the Russians seemingly as astonished as my own men.

The man on the ground was one of the two starshinas from the troop, and the highest ranking man here. Someone kicked his gun away and we turned back toward the duel, me sitting on the man's chest. Hurasu had been hit, in the thigh.

It was all the advantage Xahun needed. Hurasu was hobbling, no longer able to meet his opponent equally, only managing to defend himself. Again and again Xahun's sword batted his aside, coming within a inch or two of striking him. Blood ran down Hurasu's leg.

The dome of light had evaporated, neither bothering to maintain it, both intent on their swordplay. Another clash, and Xahun emerged with blood on his saber. Hurasu was beaten back, his long sword dangling from a seemingly nerveless hand. Xahun prepared to end it. We all knew he would.

Sossinsky stepped forward, braced himself on his crutch. He pulled his own heavy revolver from beneath his coat. Holding it steady with both hands and methodically squeezing the trigger, he fired all seven bullets into Xahun. The sorcerer looked at him, stunned, unbelieving, swaying on his feet but not yet falling. Hurasu gripped his blade and with a mighty swing took his opponent's head from his shoulders. Then both figures slumped to the ground.

So it ended.

62. Spring Will Come

Two peoples became one that afternoon, the soldiers we had been killing from ambush now our friends. What an unlikely hero had brought this about! Andri, a man of seemingly perpetual weariness, had stepped forward. A man who had said he did not know how to oppose Xahun had found that way.

What now? The people could return to their villages, the reindeer could come north and cross the hills as they had for centuries. Hurasu would go home. Soon, too, for he recovered from his wound far more quickly than an ordinary man. "We will go by boat, before the autumn storms begin," Konosi told me. "I and Ashaga and her brother, and the wizard will travel with us before going on. I shall stay in the north." This surprised me not at all.

The sorcerer invited me to come along. "A man such as you could serve in my valley," he said. "A general of my troops, and Vasa, one of the greatest of my wizards. It would make for a more pleasant journey with you along, too," he added.

"Some of the people here will want to go north as well," I reminded him. "Quite a large group, I imagine." Too many for a few skin boats.

"They would hinder me," he answered bluntly. "If you feel a duty to them, you will have to lead them forth later."

There was the question. Did I feel a duty or had that been discharged? Ah, that was not what mattered. I must speak to Vasa.

"No, Yuzi," she told me. "I will not go, now or later. This is my home, this village. These are my people and I shall serve them as their shaman. I hope you will stay with me."

I nodded slowly. I hoped so too, but I did not know. For now, I would stay here and help the new arrivals, the Russian troops find their place in these empty lands. It was too late to do anything different for them this year. But spring would come again.

Spring, and I might choose at last to go, to explore the rest of this world, the lands beyond Nagi. I kissed Vasa.

Afterword

Those who have read any of the novels in my Malvern and Mora trilogies will recognize some things in 'Tsar of the Empty Lands.' In particular, there is the ancient sorcerer Hurasu who played a major role in the second Malvern novel, 'Valley of Visions.' This book is set some years after the last Mora novel, 'Woman of the Sky,' and serves as a sort of bridge to an upcoming novel that will begin a new trilogy set among the Mora. None of these books need be read to understand any of the others, of course.

It may be we shall see a sequel to 'Tsar' as well. When? Maybe when spring comes again to the Empty Lands.

Stephen Brooke

Stephen Brooke is an author, poet, and artist, residing in an old farmhouse in the Florida Panhandles. All his books are available through the Arachis Press.

http://arachispress.com

www.ingramcontent.com/pod-product-compliance
Lightning Source LLC
Chambersburg PA
CBHW030325020726
47493CB00004B/1159